W9-AXC-678

STEP
TO THE
STARS

LESTER DEL REY

PAPERBACK LIBRARY, Inc.
New York

PAPERBACK LIBRARY EDITION

First Printing: May, 1966

To
WILLY LEY
who taught us to believe

This Paperback Library Edition is published by arrangement
with Holt, Rinehart and Winston, Inc.

Chapter 1 No Strings Attached

The floor of the big garage was bitterly cold with the first touch of winter. Jim Stanley shoved his short, stocky figure out from under the big turbine-powered car and stood up, beating his hands together to warm them. He put his tools and grease gun back on the rack and headed for the warmth of the washroom, shucking off his cap and goggles as he went.

Where the goggles had protected his face, rings of clean skin contrasted with the grease and oil smudges elsewhere, and there were still hints of freckles over his snub nose. As a kid, he'd hated the freckles even more than his carroty-red hair and the blue eyes that went with his complexion. But now he was used to his looks and didn't notice them as he began scrubbing off the grime.

"Griswold wants you," one of the other mechanics shouted at him from the doorway. "Better make it snappy, Jim. Looks like one of his bad days!"

Jim nodded and began drying his face in front of a blast of hot air. It was a bad day for Griswold most of the time, but the owner of the garage was usually fair about things, even though his disposition left much to be desired. Jim tried to think of some error he might have made, and could think of none. He shrugged and went back into the shop.

"Stanley!" Griswold was waiting by the outer door of the office, scowling. He waited until Jim reached him, and then jerked his hand back toward the office. "Stanley, there's another FBI man in there, asking about you. I thought you told me you'd never been in any trouble."

"That's right, sir. I told you before, I applied for some kind of job. And I don't know how the FBI got into it. They were around to see my landlady, too. But . . ."

Griswold grunted doubtfully. "Since when do they check up twice on job applications? I don't like it, Stanley. Don't like the FBI prowling around investigating here, taking up my time. And there's something else I don't like! How old are you?"

"Eighteen, Mr. Griswold. I never told you anything else."

The man pondered over it, and nodded doubtfully. "Maybe you didn't—but you knew blamed well I took you for a lot older. You're getting a man's wages here, and I don't pay that to kids. I can get plenty of them at half price if I want them."

"Haven't I been doing a man's work, sir?" Jim protested.

Griswold nodded again, reluctantly. "Maybe so. I'm not kicking about the work. But I don't like this whole business. Finish the job?"

He followed Jim to the big Chrysler, inspected the work sheet, and started the motor, listening to the steady purring sound it made. "Good job," he said finally. "Better'n most of the men do. Look, Stanley, I want to be fair with you. But the rest of them can't be expected to work for the same wages a kid can get. And I'm not going to have them all yelling for more pay. How much you got coming to you?"

Jim felt his face tighten, and there was a hard knot in his stomach. But if there had ever been any red-headed impulsiveness about him, he'd had it beaten out of him by other, larger boys years before. He kept his voice under control. "Four days, sir."

"Okay. Change your clothes and see what the FBI man wants. I'll have your pay check ready when you come out." He hesitated, then shrugged. "And I'll throw in a week's severance pay and give you a top letter of recommendation. Okay?"

"Thanks. I—I appreciate it." Jim tried to make it sound sincere, knowing the man was being more than fair according to his own ideas. He headed for the lockers.

The other men were staring at him as he passed, but he avoided their glances. He'd been getting along all right with them, but he hadn't made friends with anyone in particular, and he was hoping that he wouldn't have to answer any questions. Now that he was fired again, the sooner he was gone the better. Yet somehow, it hurt when none of them came into the locker room after him. He switched to his regular clothes with fumbling fingers and headed back to the office without looking at the others. One started toward him, then turned back to work. That was all.

There was a tall, rough-featured man waiting for him. The man stood up, smiling pleasantly, and held out a hand. "James Stanley? I'm John Mattern." He flipped a badge out of his wallet. "About your application . . ."

"Can't we talk about it somewhere else?" Jim asked. "I mean, I'd rather not block Mr. Griswold's office. My room's just a few blocks away."

The other nodded at once. "Sure, let's get out of here. As a matter of fact, I'm supposed to take you for an interview at the office." He hesitated for a second, clearing his throat. "Stanley, I'm sorry about what happened. If I'd known your boss didn't know your age, I'd have handled things differently. But maybe it's just as well. Your application has been getting a lot of attention."

"Yeah." Jim brushed the apology aside and managed something like a grin. "It isn't the first time I've been fired because of my age, Mr. Mattern. What kind of job is this I'm being investigated for, anyhow? I didn't think the government was mixed up in it."

"It isn't, exactly. Maybe you'd better ask about it at your interview."

Mattern was still pleasant, but he refused to say anything more. Jim collected his check on the way out, endorsed it, and waited while Griswold cashed it from the till. The garage owner shook Jim's hand briefly and wished him an automatic good luck. Then Mattern led the way to his parked car. Jim climbed in and sat watching the street without seeing it as they headed toward the heart of the city.

"We're early. Want to stop for lunch?" the FBI man asked. At Jim's assent, he swung up in front of a small steak house. It was still early enough for seats to be available.

Jim let Mattern order and asked for the same. It turned out to be sirloin. He began eating it automatically, wondering what a government job would pay to someone who had no special training. It would be less than Griswold's wages, probably. Yet with jobs harder to get the last few months, it might take too long to find another. He couldn't afford to live on his savings, if he ever intended to go back to finish his course at Central Tech. And that was something he had to do.

Jim's mother had died when he was born, and he'd always traveled with his father, who was a construction engineer. It had been tough at times, but he'd loved it, and it had been taken for granted that he had to be an engineer someday, too. Then, when his father had found a job on a government rocket project, Jim had known exactly what he wanted. He'd nearly "killed" himself forcing his way through high school in half the normal time so that he could enter the rocketry courses at Central Tech while the field was still new. With the help of some of the men on the project, he'd been admitted as the youngest freshman in his class. And a few months later, he learned that his father had been killed in the wild explosion of one of the rockets.

When the shock wore off, he found himself living with his only other relative, his mother's older brother, who had been appointed his guardian. He'd swallowed his grief and dug into his studies, swearing that he'd use the money his father had left to become an engineer his father would have been proud of. He finished the first year, came back to his uncle's house to study all through the summer, and rushed back to his courses.

The next summer, his uncle disappeared before he could return. Apparently the man had meant well, but his business had been failing, and he'd borrowed Jim's money—as well as what he could get from his friends—and had lost it all. Rather than face his nephew, he'd slipped away, leaving only a fumbling, unhappy letter and a check for the few dollars that had remained.

When college started again, Jim had been working in an airplane assembly plant. When the union discovered his age and protested, he'd found work at Griswold's. Rocketry wasn't a subject that could be studied while holding down a part-time job, and his only hope had been to save enough in one year to pay his way through his courses the next. And now . . .

He shoved the empty plate aside and followed Mattern out of the restaurant, stopping to buy a paper. He glanced at the headlines. Employment was down slightly. There were new threats of possible trouble being stirred up by the Combine, the big collection of countries occupying eastern Europe and most of northern Asia. The editorial was one of the paper's regular blasts at the administration for not building a space station. It was obvious the writer knew nothing about space stations, but was using the idea for purely political purposes. And there were no jobs that looked possible.

They were heading downtown again as Jim dropped the paper. Mattern glanced at him, and shook his head. "I feel like a heel for letting your age slip, kid. I don't blame you for being a little bitter."

"Bitter?" Jim considered it, wondering if the man was sounding him out. But it didn't matter. "I don't hate the world or anyone in it, if that's what you think. And if I'm bitter, what about everyone else?"

Mattern shrugged. "At your age, you should be bubbling with hope and idealism. I was. But now all you young men seem to be confused and uncertain. You're like a bunch of pups out in the rain, wondering if they'll ever be dry again. It's as if you still had your ideals, but they'd gone sour. What's behind it?"

"I don't know." It was an uncomfortable conversation, but it dug into Jim's mind somehow. He stirred uncertainly. "Maybe they should have built that space station!"

Mattern grunted, ending the conversation abruptly. But there was no sign to show whether the remark had scored for or against Jim. It might be a sore subject. One of the leading papers had uncovered the fact two years before that a leading industrial firm had offered to begin building a space station from completed, practical plans—if the government would give permission—and had been refused. The government had claimed the plans were impractical, while the paper and quite a few political commentators insisted it was untrue, and that the government had secretly agreed with other nations to have nothing to do with attempted space flight.

It had been a scandal for some time, and it had nearly destroyed the hopes of most people for peace and new frontiers from such a station. Those hopes had grown slowly for years, and they died hard. Even Jim's faith had been shaken. There was no reason he could see for not having a station in space already—but there was no sign of official interest in such a project.

They arrived at the Federal Building finally, and threaded their way through endless corridors and past innumerable guards to a small office. Mattern motioned Jim to a seat and went in. A few minutes later he came out, motioning Jim inside.

There were two men in the office. Mattern introduced the one in uniform as Colonel Halpern. The other, who seemed to be a gray-haired man of the type seen in the better businessmen's clubs, was introduced simply as Mr. Jonas. The colonel nodded faintly at Mattern, who left. Mr. Jonas motioned Jim to take a chair.

"Sit down, Jim. I've seen you before, though I guess you wouldn't remember."

Jim stared at him, and then blinked. The man had come into the garage with a powerful imported car and had stood around while it was repaired. Now he nodded. "Certainly, I was spying on you. You've no idea how carefully you've been checked. We even know who sent you the application form you filled in. Or did you think that was a form circulated generally? You've got friends, boy!"

"Who?" Jim asked doubtfully. He'd been puzzled to receive the application, but had finally decided that it must have been one sent to all former employees of the aircraft plant. Now it seemed he was wrong.

The colonel shook his head, and Jonas smiled cryptically. "We can skip that, Jim. And maybe you'll find out by yourself—because we've decided we can use you. Oh, if this were a routine application, we might pick someone else; after all, some of your qualifications are a bit weak. But as I said, you have friends, and there are things about you we like—things you probably don't know about yourself. That is, we've almost decided we can use you . . ."

Jim swung to the colonel. "Sir, can you tell me what this is all about?"

Jonas' face fell, but the colonel leaned back and laughed softly. "Jonas is trying to rattle you—and you don't rattle. Good. Jim, I want three questions answered as fully as you can answer them. We've checked indirectly, but we want your answers. One, do you have any friends—including girl friends—you see or correspond with regularly? Two, do you have any debts or obligations you have to meet? And three, when you were moving around with your father, we know you sometimes went up to the top of one bridge he was working on. Were you ever afraid of the height?"

Jim considered them, his head spinning. The questions made as little sense as anything else in this interview. He shrugged his shoulders, mustering a grin. "When I know what kind of job it is, I'll be glad to answer, sir."

"Suppose I told you we're considering you for two jobs —one that pays two hundred dollars a week, the other paying a great deal more?" Jonas asked, studying him with obvious amusement.

"I'd say you wouldn't get your money's worth, sir," Jim answered. "I don't have any skills worth that—unless it's a pretty dangerous job."

"It could be," the colonel said. "You'd have to sign a waiver in advance. Let's say the higher-salaried job might be dangerous, but that you wouldn't have to take it. It would be up to you. Suppose I said it had something to do with rockets?"

Jim felt something twist in his stomach. He swallowed, and the words poured out before he could think. "I—I'd say no to all three questions. No, sir."

"Absolutely no strings attached here, Jim?"

"Absolutely none, sir." He took the pen the colonel held out and signed the papers on the desk with hands that trembled a little.

The colonel folded them and put them away carefully. From a drawer he drew out a small envelope. "All right. Mattern will drive you to your room. He'll help you pack a small suitcase, and will take everything else to put in storage for you. Tell your landlady you're moving, and nothing else. Then Mattern will take you to a plane and put you aboard. You're to give this envelope to the man who meets you when you land. And don't bother opening it —it's a punched card that makes sense only to a machine. That's all. Good luck, Mr. Stanley!"

Both the colonel and Jonas shook hands with Jim before Mattern came in to take him out.

It wasn't until he was finished his hurried packing and on the way toward the airport that he began to think clearly. Then he sat up sharply, cursing himself.

"Something biting you?" Mattern asked.

Jim grinned crookedly. "I guess I did the biting," he said.

The two men in the office had told him exactly nothing. They hadn't actually said the job paid the wages they had mentioned. They hadn't really said it had anything to do with rockets. In fact, they'd managed to avoid answering, while getting him to answer them. All he knew was that they were strangely concerned with making sure that he had no strings attached—and that nobody could ever miss him after he left.

He glanced at Mattern, estimating the strength of the man. Then he shrugged. There was nothing he could do now except to go along peacefully. But what sort of mess had he gotten himself into?

Chapter 2 The Big Shush

The plane had proved to be no clue to the destination. It was one of the big, four-jet models used for carrying heavy loads at high speeds and could have been going five hundred miles or five thousand. Most of the space inside was filled with boxes and crates, but there were four seats over the wings.

Mattern handed him the magazines they'd bought, and held out a friendly hand just inside the doorway. "This is as far as I go, kid. Have a nice trip."

Jim shook hands with him, feeling he was breaking the last contact with familiarity. He headed up the aisle toward his seat, grimacing slightly. There wasn't anything that he was leaving behind which he'd miss much. As to what was coming, he'd face that when he reached it. So far, he'd always been able to take care of himself, and he was pretty sure he could handle things in the future.

The two seats on one side of the aisle were occupied, one by a big man who had the tan and calloused hands of an outdoor laborer, and the other by a thin, elderly man busy with charts in a big notebook. The other two seats were empty, and Jim dropped into the one across from the laborer. He waited until the man looked across at him and grinned in as friendly a manner as he could.

"Looks like good weather for flying," he said. "I hope it lasts all the way."

The man grunted unhappily. "You don't hope it like I do. First time they ever got me on one of these things."

"Oh? Well, I've never been on a trip this long on one either." He waited to see what the reaction to that was, but drew a blank. "I wonder what it will be like when we get there?"

The third man turned around to study Jim, and there was an amused grin on his face. "You'll find out when you

17

get there, young man," he said. "And you can stop probing. He doesn't know any more than you do."

"But I suppose you know, sir?" Jim asked with careful respect.

The grin broadened, and the man nodded. "I do," he answered, and turned back to his charts.

Jim muttered to himself, but he had to admit he'd been asking for it. Then the door of the plane was shut and locked from outside, and the big jets began roaring. He turned to the window as the ground streaked past. They rose smoothly, circling for altitude. At about eleven thousand feet they ran into a thick cloud blanket, and passed through it, to level off and begin pouring on speed. The clouds cut off all view of the ground below, and the sun had set, while there were too few stars within Jim's view for him to guess their direction. He was sure they'd headed west, however; it fitted, since most of the rocket fields lay in that direction. Maybe the colonel's hints had been true.

The man who knew where they were going had put his notebook away in a locked brief case, and now was settling down to sleep. Jim shrugged, and decided he might as well do the same. He found the catch on the seat and tipped it back all the way, realizing that such seats were seldom installed on short-range ships. He cut off his seat light, and turned over. The little hum of the air pressure system blended with the muted roar of the jets, and sleep came quickly.

The change of pressure hit at his ears and woke him up hours later as they glided down for a landing. He swallowed and stared out of the window, but could make nothing of what lay below. His watch indicated that eight hours had passed. They must be on the West Coast.

A few minutes after the landing, the door opened and a man in major's uniform stuck his head in. "You'll be here for some time while we refuel," he announced. "However, I'll have to ask you not to leave the plane. Food will be brought to you. Oh, hello, Dr. Swenmark."

"Hi, Major," the man in the front seat called back. "How

about some of the Yankee pot roast? That still on the menu?"

"Can do," the major said. The door shut behind him, and Swenmark smiled at Jim.

"I make the trip about once a week," he said. "Any idea where we're going now? If you guess it the first time, I'll admit it."

"Johnston Island," Jim said. If they were refueling here, it had to mean a long trip over the Pacific. And it wouldn't be anyplace without rockets with Swenmark on board. The man was one of the experts whose name was known to Jim from his studies at Central Tech.

Swenmark's face hardened abruptly, and he switched to the seat ahead of Jim, swiveling it round to face the boy. "How did you know about that?" he asked sharply.

"A guess. If they're working on long-range rockets in the Pacific, it has to be in United States waters—and Hawaii is too well settled. There've been rumors that Johnston Island was being used."

Swenmark relaxed, and the smile returned. "Central Tech, I'll bet? I thought so. I heard they were investigating a young man who'd studied there. Henrix still using my book in his course?"

He'd switched the conversation to safe grounds smoothly, but Jim let it drift as Swenmark wanted. He knew there *were* rockets involved in his future work now, and he stopped worrying. They discussed the school and Jim's courses while a pretty stewardess brought their food and then took the plates away. Outside, the mechanics were working on the far right jet.

When they finally took off, they ran into rough weather that pitched the plane about. The worker was violently sick. By the time Jim and Swenmark had taken care of him and cleaned up, they were cruising smoothly again. The older man went back to his charts, and Jim settled down to a halting conversation with the third man. Finally it died out, and he turned to the magazines.

Hours later, Swenmark moved over again and pointed down. The sky was clear, and the blue of the Pacific was bright below them. On it, the tiny outlines of a ship showed up—but no ship such as he had ever seen. It looked like a stubby ship that was split into a letter *U* at the rear. From it, big cranes of some kind were pulling an object into the U-section.

It could only be a vessel especially built to rescue the big first stage of a three-stage rocket, dropped off after it had used up all its fuel. Having fallen on its parachute, it would now be carried back to its base for re-use. Jim knew the theory from his studies, but he hadn't known that they were actually to the point of building and using such rockets! He looked up at Swenmark, but the man shook his head, indicating no questions were to be asked.

No more reading was possible for Jim. He knew they must be near their destination now—about two hundred or less miles away, if what he knew of the trajectory of the first stage was correct. He tried to realize that he was to see and probably to work on the true space-reaching rockets that he'd only dreamed of before.

Then he frowned. If they had them, why was it kept secret? Why leave people thinking that research was still puttering along with slightly improved V-2 rockets and getting nowhere? The mention of danger came back to him, sobering him. There must be something wrong with the whole setup, and that was probably where it lay—the big rockets were still unsafe. He was willing to take the risk, if he had to, but he didn't like the idea of being tricked into it.

They came in for a landing finally, dropping down onto the field of what must be Johnston Island, nearly a thousand miles beyond Hawaii. Almost at once, the door opened and Swenmark headed out, while two other men came in. One of them looked at the two remaining passengers and headed for Jim. "Mr. Stanley? You're to come with me."

Jim stretched gratefully when they got out, but the guide was moving toward a little three-wheeled jeep. He fidgeted impatiently as Jim swept the horizon, until the rocket field finally showed before his eyes, over the roofs of the temporary buildings.

The swell of the two ships answered his question. The ships were three-stage jobs, without any doubt.

"All right, Mr. Stanley," the guide called. "You can gawp at them later."

Jim reluctantly got into the jeep, which headed along a street outside the airfield, away from the rockets. The men along the street were about evenly divided between those wearing uniforms and those in civilian dress. He turned to the guide, with questions already formed.

Then a roar of thunder sounded, and he swiveled to stare back toward the rocket field. Over the roofs of the buildings, a monster rocket was rising slowly, teetering on a huge gout of fire. It seemed to hover at first, and then to gain sureness. Its speed increased, and the last signs of red vanished from the brilliant blue of the exhaust. With a thunder of sound that lowered in pitch as it diminished, it lifted, leaped, and rocketed upward and out of sight.

The guide looked bored, but slightly amused, at Jim's expression. He swung the jeep to a doorway, stopped, and got out. Jim followed, with the roar of the rocket still ringing in his ears. They went down a hall and into the back of the building. Three men were waiting in one of the offices. "Mr. James Stanley," the guide announced, and left.

"You've got an envelope for us," one of the men said. He was a huge bear of a man, with an accent that sounded faintly Germanic. His smile was friendly, but he seemed bored with the routine they were going through. He took the card from the envelope and handed it to another man, who put it into a huge machine at the back. "Now, young man! We will see what they've sent us this time!"

He sounded doubtful. Jim began to understand why as they threw questions at him—questions that involved everything in his life, and squeezed him dry as to his abilities. The big man was frowning as he listened to the experience Jim had had. He reached for the sheets the machine had typed out from the information on the card.

"Hmm, so! Well, you have enough friends, Mr. Stanley.

I thought so. There had to be some reason behind their sending you to us. Jonas! He should have been in politics."

"You mean I'm not hired yet?" Jim asked. "But I was told the job was definite." He should have known there would be a catch to it. A million men would have been happy to apply for any job that had to do with rockets, and he had nothing to offer beyond his own desires.

"You're hired," another man told him. "You didn't think you'd be permitted to leave here after seeing the ships, did you? You've been on salary since you signed the waiver. Now our problem is to find what to do with you."

Jim sighed and nodded. "All right. For two hundred a week and a chance to be where the ships are being flown, I don't care what you want me to do."

"Good." The big man laughed suddenly. "Very good. But suppose it isn't two hundred a week? I suppose you'll work for nothing, eh?"

"If I have anything to say about it, sir, I will not. I want to do what I can to help with the rockets, but I can't pay for an education with empty pockets."

The laughter came again, richer and more approving. "I like that, Stanley. We want men with ideals here—but we can't use fools who have their eyes filled with stars and their heads stuffed with nonsense. Well, you have some good points. You're young, you're used to work, you're un-attached—and you're about the right size. We like that when we can get it. Do you think we should test him, gentlemen?"

Jim stared at them in amazement. After weeks of being checked by the FBI and the long quiz here, it seemed to him that he'd already been tested. Apparently they didn't think so. The other two debated for a moment, and finally seemed to agree. The older one spoke for both of them. "I guess we might as well. We can use a few replacements. All right, send him in. And I hope that's all of this routine for a while."

There was another hallway, and a ride in another jeep. But this time the card was studied carefully by the man who received him. Finally he was turned over to a man who was obviously a doctor.

The doctor smiled, and studied the material from the card. "All right, Jim," he said finally. "Better take off your clothes and prepare to stay for a while. This is going to be long, rough, and probably nonsensical to you. But it's for your own good."

Some of the tests, such as the heart and blood pressure test, the check on his basal metabolism in the big chamber that measured his temperature after he ate a piece of candy, and the routine check, made some sense. He was X-rayed, examined for scars, and had the inside of his eyes, ears, and nose studied with strange instruments. He was put on a whirling table and spun until he was too dizzy to stand—and then ordered to stand up, while a doctor kept a record with a stop watch.

At first he'd counted on being done in a few hours. But he soon learned better. The medical examination took most of a day, and that was only the beginning. There was a psychologist who put ink blots in front of him and asked what he saw. He answered innumerable questions. He did things with blocks and holes, memorized nonsense syllables, and was pronounced an ectomorph, an introvert, a normal, and other things he couldn't understand.

The second day was better. He was given work to do with a welder, and had to learn by experience that the piece marked Mild Steel was actually stainless. They seemed approving when he guessed that another wasn't aluminum, but a magnesium alloy, and insisted on welding it in an atmosphere of an inert gas. Most of that was familiar from what he'd seen in the aircraft plant. But he was totally unfamiliar with the next test.

They had him climb up fifty feet inside a tower, walk out on a narrow beam, and try to bolt together a meaningless collection of parts that hung on strings just out of reach. He demanded and got a safety belt for that. From the reaction on their faces, he suspected that it had been partly a trap, and that he'd have flunked if he hadn't asked for the belt, even though there was a thin nylon net below him. They gave him a rest then, and sent him into a big centrifuge—a little cabin at the end of a big boom which was swung in a circle by a huge motor until the outward pressure made him feel that he weighed ten times as much as before. Then they sent him back to finish his medical tests.

It was three days later when he went into a small office and found the big man he'd first met on the Island. There was a smile on the man's face again, and he held out his hand.

"You've passed, Jim. Oh, there's a lot that isn't all we want. But you just qualify, and your friends have done you no harm. Your professor at Central Tech practically forced us to consider you. Swenmark turned in a good word, too."

"So I can work on the rockets?" Jim asked. He hadn't dared to think about it too much, but he wasn't fool enough to think that all those tests were needed for a simple mechanic. "Do you think I can learn to handle them?"

"Not so fast." The man sat down, studying him. "I don't know about that, Jim. We have plenty of pilots who are better fitted than you are. No, you won't be working on the ships. Did you ever hear of the Big Shush?"

"No, sir. But . . ."

"Ever wonder why we didn't build a space station when that eager-beaver company volunteered?"

"Yes, sir." They must know the answer to that.

The man took a deep breath, and his voice sounded unbelieving. "Well, Jim—it was because we were already working on one here. The Big Shush is a space station. And you're going to work on it, if you are willing to take the risk." His voice softened, and his eyes turned toward the rocket field. "We're finally in space, Jim."

Jim saw tears in the man's eyes. His own eyes were curiously blurred as he tried to realize what had happened to him.

Chapter 3 Space Station One

The wages Jim was to receive were almost as fabulous as the job: the starting salary was fifteen hundred a month plus all his living expenses. He'd gotten used to the idea that jobs in out of the way places involving high risks paid far more than the usual work, but this was more than he had dared to think of. And since it carried a guarantee of six months of work if he lasted for two weeks, it meant he'd be able to save enough to return to Central Tech without future worries.

He signed waivers to protect his employers in case of accident, and documents attesting that he was going of his own desire. The name of the company building the station was one he had seen all his life—Major Electric Company —and he discovered that it was a private contract, with government supervision.

Then for two days he was fitted for clothes made of the thinnest and lightest material, and for a space suit that would protect him from the vacuum of space. That couldn't be light, no matter how important weight saving was on a rocket. He was taught how to handle his air supply, the method of sealing it, and to avoid tearing the fabric. He was lectured on everything that could be told about working conditions outside the atmosphere and without any effective gravity.

In the two days of that, he had time to adjust to some extent. One sobering fact helped to keep him from losing his head. He was warned that all they could do was to send him up. Whether he stayed would depend on his own ability to adapt. Only about one man in three could adjust. It meant that his chances were not even fifty-fifty.

He gritted his teeth with his determination to stay at least the minimum ten days. And then he berated himself for thinking of the money while he should be planning to do and die for glory. But he'd had too much experience with the need of a cushion of savings, and too little with whatever glory might be.

Finally, though, he was ready. He was dressed in one of the two sets of coveralls and soft, insulating under-clothes he'd take with him, his space suit was folded over his arm, and he had all his other permitted possessions in one pocket. There was even a special wrist watch, made out of light plastics, and he had been sweated down to seven pounds less than usual. The cost of fifteen dollars a pound for the trip was less important than the need to carry as much useful cargo as possible each time.

He was taken out to the field and had his first full view of the big ships. Three were in. The one on which he was scheduled to go stood ready, resting on a huge platform that held the exhaust deflectors to handle the first blast, before the ship could rise. It was already fueled with hydra-zine and nitric acid, and the hydrogen peroxide which would drive the fuel pumps was in the tanks. It needed only a spark to start.

The ship stood on its base, the first stage. This was over sixty feet in diameter and one hundred and twenty feet in length. It was equipped with huge fins which would stabi-lize it for its short passage through the denser air. Coupled to that was the second stage, forty-five feet in diameter and nearly seventy in length. As against the seven thousand tons of the first stage when fueled, the total weight of the second stage was a mere thousand tons.

Rising above the rest was the final stage—the rocket that would actually get out into space. It was only about twenty feet across, and its length of not quite eighty feet tapered up to a needle point that stood two hundred and sixty-five feet above the ground. Its base was equipped with two wings which would be used on the return trip, and its nose held the steering stabilizers. Complete with cargo and fuel, it weighed about one hundred and forty tons.

Jim was staring up at its dizzy height, awed by the bulk of what had been only figures on paper before, when he felt a hand on his shoulder and was swung around to face a small, slim man who seemed to be all whiplash and whale-bone. "Welcome, spaceman!"

"Mark Emmett!" Jim caught the other's hand and pumped it furiously. Emmett had been his favorite assistant instructor in the first-year courses at Central Tech. He'd exploded through the courses like a meteor, but with a sound, clear sense of exactly what should be said to make the hardest problem clear. The thin silk shirt and brief shorts of a rocket pilot somehow went with him, as did the crew cut over his still boyish features. "You—you're the one who sent me that application!"

The pilot grinned. "Who else? Didn't I tell you we'd live to hit space together? Come on aboard, and see how it feels!"

A lift wheeled up to them. It was similar to a multi-sectioned fire ladder mounted on a wheeled base. Now the ladders were all down, and the little platform that slid along them was at ground level. Jim followed Mark onto it, and it began wheeling forward toward the rocket, while the platform ran up to the top. The ladders began cranking upward, each adding its length to the others until they were swaying dizzily halfway up the length of the ship.

It moved in closer, and Mark caught a rope and aluminum ladder that stretched down from above. He moved onto it easily, and turned to help Jim. But the boy had mastered rope ladders years before on the bridgework, and he climbed up after the pilot, glad that he didn't need assistance. It swayed under their weight, but they swarmed up the ship. The ground crew became mere dots below them. Finally, they were at the crew hatch in the third stage, near the top.

The hatch was thinner than Jim had expected. He'd unconsciously pictured the heavy air locks of the movies, but this was a circle made of light metal, braced with struts. Mark pulled it shut by hand, and secured it with a series of clamps. Three feet beyond, another door opened inward, equally light. They went through, and shut it. "Air pressure inside would hold it closed," Mark said. But he snapped the locks and tested them, anyhow. "The hatches seal against silicone rubber, so they're airtight."

They went through a small tunnel, and up a narrow ladder into the control cabin at the nose of the ship. The copilot and radioman were already seated in contour chairs heavily padded with foam rubber and mounted to swing in all directions.

"Jim Stanley, this is Lee Yeng." Mark pointed to the copilot, a smiling Chinese-American. He turned to the radarman. "And this is Hank Andrucci. They know about you. Here, I've saved the best seat for you, up by me. You can see all the screens."

He pointed to the seat, and Jim sank into it, buckling himself in with wide, soft webbing straps. There were banks of radar and television screens there; windows in a space ship were out of the question, since they would have required bulky metal shields when making the high-speed return through the atmosphere. Small television cameras were lighter, also, with the transistors that had replaced most of the older electron tubes. Each screen was marked, and he tried to memorize the location. The side ones were already on, showing the bustle of activity in full color.

Most of the cabin was taken up with various machinery that hummed and clicked. There was almost no waste space. Mark patted one of the machines fondly. "Here's your real pilot, Jim. Under acceleration, no man can function well—and things have to be done more precisely than a man could do them. The whole course is here in these gadgets—they pilot all the way, except in emergencies. It gives me the easiest job in the world. We take off in three minutes. Better lie back and relax."

It began as a muted mutter that rose to a roar. In the screen, Jim could see fumes of fuel run out, then ignite into a harsh red that gradually turned blue. The great ship stirred slowly and began to lift, only a few feet the first second, but gaining speed. It teetered uncertainly, while the full power of its fifty-one rocket motors bellowed out behind. Then pressure began to build as the acceleration increased. Jim was shoved back deeper and deeper into his seat. At first it was no more than the pressure of an express elevator starting. Then his weight seemed to double, and to build up until the breath was nearly squeezed from his lungs. He felt the muscles of his face and body pull back like melting wax, and his sight began to blur. He could barely see that the ship was turning from its upward course and leveling out to a path that was only about twenty degrees from horizontal.

"There goes the first stage," Mark shouted a minute and a half after take-off. There was a halt in acceleration pressure as the burned-out first stage was blown free by a charge of powder, to go falling back to Earth on its parachute. They should already be thirty miles from take-off, twenty-five miles up and doing about five thousand miles an hour. The second stage began firing almost instantly, its smaller blast working against less weight with the huge first stage gone. He suffered through the pressure for more than two minutes this time.

"Second stage out," Mark called. It, too, was blasted out, to drop in the ocean eventually, nearly a thousand miles from the Island and be recovered. They were hurtling along at fourteen thousand miles an hour, already hundreds of miles around the Earth.

The final stage went into operation. It was the rocket proper, the section that carried the cargo and men to their destination. For another minute and a half, it blasted them savagely ahead, before the automatic pilot cut it off. There was still fuel left, but they had reached their maximum speed of eighteen thousand miles an hour. In five minutes, they had come seven hundred miles and had risen more than sixty miles above the Earth. Now they were rising slowly, heading out to space!

There was no feeling of weight now. Earth's gravity still pulled them downward, but since it acted on the ship as much as on the men, it couldn't be felt. They went on rising on their momentum, and would continue upward, losing speed under the pull of that gravitiy—men and ship alike.

Jim had expected something unusual, but it felt almost natural—like lying in a warm pool of water, just barely

29

floating. He turned his head, and dizziness struck at him: there was nothing to keep the fluid in place in the inner canals of his ears, and it was that fluid which gave a sense of balance. He fought against the dizziness as he had been taught, using a fixed point in front of his eyes to maintain his relation with his surroundings. The feeling slowly faded, though his hand clung to the restraining strap for reassurance.

Mark Emmett had been watching him closely. The pilot now let out a slow sigh of relief. "Praise be, Jim, you don't get space-sick. When that happens up here, it's pretty messy. Feel okay?"

"Not bad," Jim said. He was beginning to see some reason for the tests he had undergone.

There was nothing to see on the screens except for the hazy globe of Earth slowly growing smaller as they rose. A hum sounded in the cabin as the gyroscopes began to turn the ship under the maneuvering of the automatic pilot. It had no effect on the movement of the ship through space, but only served to swing the ship on its axis, to bring the rockets around, pointed where they would have to be. According to Newton's law of motion, every action was balanced by an equal and opposite reaction; the eighty tons of the ship would turn once for thousands of turns of the gyroscope's few pounds. It was cheaper than trying to steer with side rockets.

Their speed had fallen to fourteen thousand miles an hour when they reached the station orbit at 1,075 miles up. To keep from falling back toward Earth, they needed a speed of just under sixteen thousand. Now the rockets went on for fifteen seconds, adding the needed speed.

"Station two miles ahead," Lee Yeng reported. He waited while Mark fed figures into the automatic pilot. There was a weak blast, a pause, and another. "Nice going, Mark! We're here!"

It had taken fifty-six minutes altogether to bring them to a stable orbit around Earth, like that of the distant Moon, neither rising nor falling. Centrifugal force from their motion held them out, like a stone swung on a string, exactly hard enough to balance the downward pull of gravity.

Mark grabbed a space suit out of a locker. "We'll unload when I get back, boys. Jim, I'll swim you over."

The suit was of airtight fabric, with thick-soled boots and a helmet something like a diver's; on the back was an oxygen tank for breathing. It used pure oxygen at three pounds of pressure. Earth had air at fifteen pounds, but eighty per cent of that was useless nitrogen which added weight without any use. On the rocket, they had slowly switched to the low-pressure, pure oxygen atmosphere, and Jim's lungs were used to it. It saved much of the strain on the suit and avoided all danger of painful "bends" from nitrogen bubbles in the blood.

The inner seal of the air lock opened, and swung shut behind them. Pumps began hissing, pulling the air out of the lock, while all sounds faded. Then the outer seal opened. "Grab my shoulders and hang on," Mark ordered. He braced his feet against the edge of the door, aimed himself, and kicked off, out into nothingness!

The ship slipped away from them. Below lay the hazy ball of Earth and to the side was the leaping, burning flame of the Sun. Around them was—vacuum! Jim's stomach lurched and sweat popped onto his forehead. He dug his fingers into Mark's shoulders to keep from screaming. He could feel himself falling, falling . . .

He fought it out. Logically, he knew they couldn't fall, and the hours he'd spent working on girders as a kid helped. He had to think of space as a great ocean that buoyed him up. He forced himself to see Earth as a ball floating with him. Floating!

It worked. He took a deep breath, relaxed, and was himself again.

Mark bent his head back to touch helmets with Jim, and his muffled voice came through. "Space station one ahead."

Jim looked, excitement rising in him. But all he could see was a collection of metal parts, boxes and crates of machinery scattered about like toys on a nursery floor. Ahead of them lay a big metal cylinder, perhaps forty feet

31

long and thirty feet in diameter, with a skeleton of girders sticking out from each end, bent to form part of a circle. Around it floated collections of meaningless stuff, connected by thin cords, with little figures of space-suited men here and there in a meaningless pattern. It wasn't a space station, but a cosmic dumping ground!

"That's a space station?" he asked incredulously. It looked not at all like the pictures he had seen. Nothing could have been a bigger letdown.

Mark chuckled. "That's the beginning. It beats living in a rocket. You're lucky this is the fourteenth trip instead of the first."

The leap had carried them to the right of the air lock on the cylinder, but Mark caught a handhold and pulled them to the entrance. They passed through the outer door, waited for air pressure to build up, and went through the inner door, into a room walled off with thin sheets of metal. Mark threw back his helmet and yelled, his voice echoing hollowly in the air that smelled as stale as a schoolroom after the class was over.

"Hey, Dan! New fish. Come and get it!"

A figure scarcely five feet high with shoulders nearly as wide shot into view. The man's head was completely bald, though his flat face seemed no older than thirty. He spotted Jim, and his mouth split into a wide grin, while one huge paw went out.

"Dan Bailey!" Jim caught the hand, bumping against the low ceiling of the partitioned room as he leaped. He felt himself pulled down, but hardly noticed. Bailey had been his father's assistant and closest companion for years. He must have been another of the friends working to get Jim up here. "Dan!"

"You young baboon! You crazy young idiot!" Dan's voice boomed in the room, while his hands squeezed on Jim's. Then his face sobered, and he shook his head. "Jim, it's good to see you. But I'm afraid this is no favor to you. It's a tough job, boy! Look."

Two men had come in, holding a third who was wearing a space suit and bound with webbing straps. The bound man saw the air lock and began screaming and writhing as they carried him out.

"He's going back," Dan said unhappily. "Three days here, and he's gone to pieces. That's space! When three come up and only two go back, we're lucky. Space!" He made it sound like a curse.

One out of three! Jim shivered. The wonder and the glamour he'd expected seemed to have evaporated out into the great, unfriendly emptiness that stretched endlessly around them.

Chapter 4 Operation Misfit

In Dan's office the foreman dug out a chart and consulted it briefly while Jim stared at the walls where furniture seemed to pop up everywhere. It was hard to get used to the idea that there was no floor or ceiling here.

"You'll share quarters with Bart Smith," Dan decided. "Come on and I'll show you."

He bent forward and jumped casually through the doorway, to go sailing down the narrow hall, guiding himself with a touch of his hand to the wall. Jim braced himself and tried to do the same. He had to keep reminding himself that he was floating, not falling, but he managed to keep behind Dan in a series of bumping glides.

The quarters turned out to be a small room, six feet on a side, completely bare except for the canvas walls which held a few big pockets. Dan grinned at him, pointing to a set of straps on one wall. "Stow your duffle in the pockets and strap down with these to sleep, so you won't bother Bart. The bathroom's down the hall."

It was even more nonstandard. Without weight, everything had to be handled in covered containers or fastened down. Liquids were even harder to handle. The bath consisted of a plastic bag into which a man crawled, leaving his head out. The water could be sucked out after use. For other washing, a carefully dampened sponge served; it was squeezed out in a similar bag. There was no shortage of water; in fact, the body burned some of the food to carbon dioxide and water, giving off more of the liquid than was drunk, and all of it could be recovered and distilled. But handling it was difficult.

Jim studied it, realizing how much preliminary work must have been done. It might not look like much of a station, but he was beginning to realize that the begining was genuine enough. It was hard to believe after all the years of staring at the sky, knowing men could get there, and waiting until it seemed that nothing would ever be done. "The greatest thing in all our history," he said bitterly. "And they keep it a tightlocked secret. You'd think they were ashamed of progress!"

"I suppose they should take newsreels!" Dan shook his head slowly. "Don't you read the papers, boy? We're having enough trouble keeping out of war with the Combine now. Let them get wind of this and they'd figure it was an act of war. They'd swear we were putting this up for the sole purpose of carrying atom bombs over their heads. And then there would be trouble! Maybe we'd have that war. Once we get her finished, they won't dare do anything. But until then, we'd better keep it secret. Of course, if the World Congress had any real power . . ."

Dan was right, Jim realized. The World Congress, like other international bodies that had been set up to keep peace and order, had been unable to control the separate nations. He wondered, though, whether even war wouldn't be easier on the people below than the feeling that science had betrayed them by giving them horrible weapons but nothing to hope for the future. This would at least be proof that they could hope. "How long until it's finished, Dan?" he asked.

"A year from the date we started, so our contract says. And we'd better finish in time. There's a penalty clause Major Electric can't afford, if we don't." Dan reached for his helmet and began zipping up his space suit. "Time I got out and supervised the new cargo. It's a nuisance having something drift off because nobody tied it to the rest."

Jim reached for his own helmet. He had no love for the idea of going back into the nothingness of space again, but it was part of his job, and he'd better get used to it. "Want me to handle cargo, or do I start with something else?"

"You stay right here until you get used to moving without weight," Dan told him firmly.

"I don't want any special treatment," Jim protested. "If

35

I make it, fine. If I don't—well, nobody's going to fire me for my age this time, at least."

Dan chuckled, then sobered. "Like that, eh? Okay, you won't get any favors. But you'll still stay here today. Look, Jim, when I first came up, there was a guy named Joe with me. The first day he spotted some cargo drifting off and leaped for it. Put out a hand to grab it—and, naturally, when his arm moved one way his body moved the other. His suit hit a sharp edge of metal. A man dies fast out here when the air runs out of his suit, and it's not a pretty thing to see. You stay inside."

Jim practiced dutifully, gaining some proficiency as he did. He had to learn by experience that the twitch of a foot at the wrong moment could throw him off balance. Once he sneezed and was shocked to find himself sailing rapidly toward the opposite wall. But Dan nodded approvingly when he came back.

Jim was near the lock when the work shift came in. They were an odd crew. Most of them were small, since a smaller man weighed less and used slightly less food and oxygen, though a few were at least six feet in height. Some looked like college freshmen and others had the rough cocksureness of men who had sweated out a living on other construction jobs. A big, dark-complexioned man of the latter type took one look at Jim and motioned him over.

"Kid, there's trouble. You go find Dan and tell him Bart Smith said the ground jerks sent up the wrong size again. Have him give you a couple of pipestretchers—the big ones."

Jim let his expression match the seriousness of the man who would be his roommate. "Yes, sir. What grade of stretching oil do you want? And how about some prefabricated holes?"

Bart stared at him for a second, while the other men broke into laughter. Then the big face stretched into a grin, and he dropped one hand approvingly onto Jim's shoulder. "You're all right, kid. I thought you were one of the college grunts they're sending up from the rocket courses to learn space. We'll get along fine, though." He grinned as some of the younger faces turned red, then cocked his ear as a bell sounded. "Come on, chow's on."

It was a strange meal. Food was served in covered plates that were magnetically fastened to the steel table, or on skewers. Liquids came from plastic squeeze bottles.

One of the men whose face had reddened was apparently still worrying about the crack against college men. He swung toward the big man, brandishing a fork angrily. "Bart, can't you lay off ever? What's wrong with college? How else are we going to learn enough to fly the rockets?"

"Not a thing, Buster," Bart said cheerfully. "If I'd had the money, I'd have gone to college myself. But don't think there's anything wrong with a man who knows how to work, either." He chewed on a piece of meat thoughtfully, then shrugged. "And don't think it'll always be like it is now. You know how they'll teach rockets? They'll start kids at high-school age where they're still adaptable. They'll bring them out here and give them experience along with all that theory. 'Smatter, kid, you sick?"

Jim shook his head. "I'm all right," he denied. But he shoved up from the table and pushed out through the doorway into the hall, with Bart's words ringing in his ears. The man was absolutely right. Age counted in space—he'd been picked largely because he was only eighteen. A few older men, like Dan, could take it. But in the future, people wouldn't take chances. They'd start the rocket men young, and they'd start them in space.

Courses would take longer, too, as a result of what would be learned from practice. By the time he could finish his education, he'd probably be nearly twenty-five, and too old!

His only chance lay in getting the experience here—if he could stay on, where fewer than one man in three could make the grade. He had to be one who could—and he kept remembering the doubt with which he'd been passed.

He was still practicing when Bart found him later. "Come on, kid," he said. "Time to sack in. Dan tells me you go to work tomorrow and I'm to be your lead man. Can't have you so tired you'll fall off and break your neck on the rocks!"

Jim managed to laugh at the joke, as he was expected to. He felt grateful to Dan for putting him under Bart. But once he had strapped himself down to keep from drifting, sleep was a long time coming, and it was full of dreams of falling.

Next morning Bart took him to a big chart in the office to give him some idea of what they were building. It looked like a lot of the pictures Jim had seen. There was to be a great doughnut wheel about two hundred and fifty feet in diameter, of which the "hut" was the first section. That would be connected to a central hub by two hollow spokes. Their present job was to extend the girders that would form the frame for the outer structure.

Work began with a briefing in which they studied a tissue-thin blueprint of the day's expected operations. Dan laid out the rough details, and the lead men filled them in, giving each man a run-down on what would be done during the shift. Each had a tiny radio transmitter and receiver connected to his helmet, but the power was so low that it could only reach a few hundred feet. They were supposed to require as few instructions on the job as possible.

Jim's job turned out to be running a small welder that operated on compressed oxygen and acetylene. "You'll be working on some tricky alloys," Bart told him. "Keep the oxygen supply a little under what you need for the best burning. And before you turn it on, get a good grip. It's a small rocket, and don't forget that!"

They filed out. Some of the men seemed to be fully at home already, and simply dived off into space, kicking themselves toward the work. They carried tiny rocket tubes which could be used to kick themselves back in case they misjudged, but it wasn't something Jim cared to try yet. He was glad to see that others pulled themselves along the girders hand over hand.

Everything seemed to be done by hand power. Men were moving out to the piles of material scattered about, sorting them, and attaching cords before pulling them back by hand. There was no weight, but the inertia of the objects sometimes required the power of several men to overcome it. Once in motion, anything tended to keep that motion, and jockeying the parts into place and holding them there was a tricky business.

The welding proceeded well enough, however. Out here without air, the metals could never tarnish. They were given a brightening before being assembled to remove any corrosion from Earth's atmosphere, and then remained bright until they would be welded. Even aluminum and the titanium alloys were manageable.

Bart came over after a few minutes and inspected his work. "Good enough. But don't sit facing the same way so long. That Sun's hotter than you think. Sit too long in one direction and you'll heat one side of your suit near melting, while the other side freezes stiff. How do you feel?"

Jim had almost stopped thinking about that, under the pressure of the work. A boy who'd collapsed on the previous shift had put the welding behind the assembly, and Jim was driving himself to catch up. Bart clapped him on the shoulder and started to move on. Then he swung back.

"Jim, don't ever let me find you with your belt unfastened on the job again!" He snapped the siliconeplastic strap around the girder and to a hook in the suit. "I told you that torch was a small rocket! Let go, and you'll sail out like a bird if you're not strapped down."

"I guess I forgot this time," Jim admitted. "Sorry, Bart!"

The other nodded. "Okay, I expect you to be a fool once. But not twice! Next time I find it that way, I kick you off and watch you try to blast back!"

He went on his way, leaving Jim's face burning. But Bart had been right, and the boy knew it. He'd been trying to work too fast, and getting careless. Like any man on a dangerous job, he'd started out being overcautious, and then had gotten cocky. Until the right habits became automatic, he'd have to watch everything.

Later, when the welding had nearly caught up, Bart put him to bolting down. That proved to be tougher. He had to handle his tools through heavy gloves. The material was either too hot from sunlight or too cold where it had been in the shadow. He had to fumble into a tight bag without letting any of the bolts escape, find a bolt and a nut, force the metal parts firmly together with a spikelike awl through the holes, and then bolt it down. The final operation was to spread the end of the bolt with a special hammer so that the nut couldn't work off.

Each blow of the hammer was a test of his skill. He had to keep insulating pads between himself and whatever he was sitting on or clinging to. These had a habit of slipping, and there was no firmness to anything. The least motion of his arms made his body shift unless he was set just right for it, and that would throw the hammer off. The sharp cone at the end had to hit exactly in the center of the bolt to spread it.

He studied the others, but no one else seemed to be doing the work where he could see. Finally he called Bart on the radio.

The man came over in a few minutes and listened while Jim outlined his troubles. Then he nodded. "Okay. And you did right. I figured you'd probably had some experience at this. My fault. I should have done what you did—ask when I didn't know." He reached for his belt and strapped it around the strut, taking Jim's hammer. Bart twisted to the side, putting the thick soles of his boots against it and snapping out against the belt. "Watch!"

He caught another piece quickly with the awl, took a bolt and nut from Jim, and snapped them in, spinning the nut on with sure fingers, and pulling it tight with a wrench. The hammer came up and down once, and it was done. "See? Don't think you have to keep pointing up from Earth. Switch over however's best—and make a tripod of your legs and belt. Then you can lever it."

It went better after that—until Jim was switched to assembling. He welcomed the chance to learn all the work being done, knowing that Bart was doing the changing deliberately. Another man was muscling the parts to him, small I-beams with ends cut to lock into others. For the first few, he had no trouble, though making them stop without long seesawing was tricky.

Then he ran into trouble. He could get them to seat halfway, but they refused to go further. The man bringing the beams went on until the right number were strung out, all lashed together by cords, and then took off on his hand-rocket for other work. The men in the crew passed on, leaving Jim behind. At last he called Bart again, but apparently the lead man was out of reach of the tiny radio.

Jim stopped to measure the ends of the beams with the catchplates into which they fitted. The top of the plate matched—but the bottom was too small. It should have been a straight groove, but it obviously wasn't. He fought on, trying to force them home, repeatedly being saved by his belt. But he couldn't get the knack, in spite of the evidence from finished work that others before him had succeeded.

Bart came over later. "Quitting time, kid," he said.

The lead man ran his eye over the incompleted work and paced back to where Jim had begun—a pitifully small distance. He came back, walking the beam by throwing his belt ahead and using it to hold himself down. He sighted along the work again.

Jim opened his mouth to explain, and then closed it. Out here, he was sure, work had to speak for itself. His didn't do much talking.

Bart made no comment as they went back, but Jim could see the frown in the man's eyes. He was surprised when Dan made no mention of his work at dinner, but Jim didn't stick around to wait for the decision. He left the men busily kidding with the girl who apparently was the nurse here and went to his quarters where they couldn't see him sweating it out.

He'd accepted the fact that he might not be able to take space—but he hadn't expected to find that he couldn't do the work. If he were washed up, it was his own fault!

Chapter 5 A Little Sunlight

Jim wasn't surprised when he found a slip by his breakfast plate. He picked it up worriedly, and read the typing there. It was an order to report to the nurse. He'd already gathered that the nurse was named Nora Prescott, and that there had been two doctors up already, neither of whom had been able to stand space. Until one could be found, she was both the only woman and the only medical help on the station. He left his breakfast unfinished and headed toward her quarters at the rear, near those of the project engineer.

His muscles ached almost as badly as his thoughts. He miscalculated the shove out of the hallway into her office, and went sprawling into her desk, to lift himself awkwardly and face her.

Nora wasn't beautiful, though she was easy enough to look at. She was smaller than Jim, and too thin for beauty. Her hair had been cut to half an inch in length, to avoid having it bush up around her head without weight to hold it down. Her nose was too short, her upper lip a bit too long, and it was hard to tell whether her eyes were green or blue. But her smile was the nicest Jim had seen.

She helped him to a better position with an ease and grace none of the men had. "You'll get used to space, Jim," she said easily. "That is, if you're in condition to work today."

"Work?" he asked stupidly. "But I thought . . ."

She stared at him quizzically, then smiled again. "All the new men have to have checkups. It doesn't mean a thing, unless I find something wrong. And you wouldn't want to work if you're not able, would you?"

He didn't disagree with her, though he had his own opinion. He waited while she took his pulse, blood pressure, and reactions to hammer taps at the knee. "Any trouble with itching inside your suit?" she asked.

It had bothered him, but he had managed to overcome it. The knowledge that he couldn't scratch had exaggerated the normal small pricklings of his skin, and only by digging into his work had it been possible to forget. He debated what to answer, and then told the truth. "Some."

She nodded. "Good. That's normal. Okay, Jim, you can report to work. It looks as if you may make it."

He couldn't believe it until he handed her slip to Dan, who looked it over and grinned. "Okay, boy. Go out and help Bart again."

Bart met him, walking him along the span of work until they came to the welder. Jim could see that another man was working on the assembly, seemingly having no trouble with the beams that had refused to fit for him. They passed that section, just as the man began fighting one of the I-beams.

"Won't fit!" he reported to Bart.

"Let it go and find one that will. I'll have the misfits collected later," Bart told him. He shook his head as they went on, his voice sounding tinnily in Jim's earphone. "I dunno. I guessed you'd run into misfits last night. There are too many of them! I've been wondering if it's sabotage on Earth. We had some trouble before with food that wasn't safe. If those darned Combine spies know about this project . . ."

He let it go. Jim took a deep breath inside his suit and raged at himself. He should have reported it. He'd been sweating it out for nothing, because he was too stubborn to admit things were going badly. And the frowns he had seen hadn't been at his work, after all. He'd been told at the aircraft plant that his work was good, but that he tried to depend too much on himself and not enough on co-operation with others. He'd insisted on doing the full job on the cars at Griswold's, even when another man could have saved him a lot of work. Now it was time he stopped being a fool.

The welding went on for several hours, until he finished what was ready. Part of the time, he'd been within reach by radio of one of the young college boys, and had struck up a conversation, forcing himself to stop being a lone wolf. He'd found that there was a sound reason for using the oxyacetylene welder instead of an electric rig. The compressed gases were lighter than batteries, and the station was still underpowered. They'd put up a sun mirror out of sheets of station walls and had used sections of pipe to make a boiler where the heat converged. It was driving a small steam plant and generator, but there were only about ten kilowatts to power the whole station until they could get the main power plant going much later.

Jim turned to find Bart, but stopped as he spotted a rocket coming up from Earth. Seeing it was like a breath of home in these alien surroundings. It crept up almost alongside and the hot exhaust shot out for a few seconds while it matched speed. But now it was over a mile away. There was another blast and still another. At the end, it was over a mile and a half from them.

Bart was standing with Dan, watching it. The foreman shrugged his shoulders. "Lousy piloting. Mark's the only one who worries about us. Well, we've got the taxi now, anyhow. Send Jerry Wales out, Bart. Hi, Jim—you all finished? Good. You might as well go along. Do you good, and there's work enough."

Jerry was a slim man of about twenty-one, with a tense, bitter face and a grin that seemed forced. But he took Jim in tow and headed back toward the hut. Jerry was a genius at moving about out of gravity. He watched Jim's face, and grinned tautly as they landed precisely in the air lock. "Used to be with a circus until my folks got killed. Aerialist. Once you get the feel, it sticks. Come on, we'll walk around to the taxi."

There were guidelines on the outside of the hut, and they grabbed these, using them as anchors to hold themselves against the outside while moving around the structure. At the rear, they came to the taxi, which Jim hadn't seen before.

The taxi looked like a huge, short salami, twenty feet long and eight in diameter. There was a small dome for the pilot to see out, and an air lock at the front, while the rear carried a small rocket motor. They went through the lock. Inside were two seats, fuel tanks, and steering assembly, as well as cargo space.

Jerry blasted off, after cranking a hand gyroscope to turn them. It was a weak, cautious blast that used little fuel. "Better to take your time and not waste fuel," he explained. "Once you get moving, there's nothing to stop you."

They drifted toward the rocket, turning over by the use of the gyroscope, and Jerry brought them to a stop with a single quick blast of the rocket tube. It was precise, beautiful work. They coasted a few feet away, while he turned them over again until the nose pointed to the rocket's lock, which was open.

"Slip your helmet back on, Jim," Jerry ordered. "Go out into the lock and catch that rope."

The man in the ship ahead had already thrown the cord. Jim found the end and fastened it to a bite inside the lock. The taxi was pulled up to the main lock, where it fitted snugly against the silicone-rubber gasket to make an airtight seal.

There were two new men this time, both looking sick from the trip up. With them was a young man whom Jerry introduced. "Jim, this is Mr. Thorndyke, our project engineer. Been down trying to get things straightened out."

They took the passengers back, and then began making trips to ferry the supplies. These were dumped out of the big rocket by the pilot and his men. Apparently they put on space suits, evacuated the air from the cargo section and lock, and simply pitched the crates and pieces into space. It was Jim's job to go out of the taxi and secure these with cords to a ring on the back of the taxi, leaving enough distance so the rocket blast wouldn't hurt them.

He began to get the feel of space slowly. The trick was always to use the smallest amount of effort, and to make no unnecessary move. It wasn't too hard to jump to whatever he was aiming for, carrying the rope, nor to slip back the rope into the taxi. They pumped the air back to leave the lock permanently open and worked in their suits.

45

At the proper places near the station, other men un-hitched the supplies and began fastening them into place. Jim saw Dan and Bart come out, using their rocket tubes for a long jump, to begin opening one of the crates that held catchplates. Apparently they were running low on them, and it was holding up the work.

After the final trip, the big rocket turned over slowly and began blasting back away from the orbit, slowing it-self to a speed of about fourteen thousand miles an hour, where it would begin drifting toward Earth again. Jim watched it go with a feeling of relief. It was hard to believe that he wasn't going to be on it, sent back in disgrace to pick up some routine work around the rocket field, with his chance at space gone forever. He reminded himself that it was still too early to be sure, but every day here was so much progress.

He had a new reason for staying now. If he could ever get a chance to use the taxi, it would be almost as good as piloting one of the rockets up from Earth . . .

Jerry cut off his thoughts. "Okay, Jim, thanks. I'll leave you here and put the taxi back. Tell Bailey it's low on fuel and I'm filling it again."

Jim hesitated on the pile of material where he stood. It was nearly half a mile to the group at work on the frame-work. He considered making the jump. Finally he shook his head and began hauling himself along the connecting cables.

Bart handed him a pile of the catchplates when he got back, and nodded toward the end of the structure. "Better start bolting these on, Jim—you know how they go now."

He found a bag of bolts, the necessary tools, and headed to the end of the extension, letting them float along at the end of the cord behind him. They had swung around Earth to face into the Sun, as they did every two hours, and he had to hold his head down to keep the savage glare out of his eyes. The faceplate of his helmet was equipped with a filter, but it wasn't enough.

He found the end of the work and began fitting the plates to it. He dogged them in with his pick and ran in

46

the first bolt, setting all within reach at first, before finishing up the bolting. Then he went back and began lining them up.

Or trying to line them up. The catchplates had the right number of holes, and in what seemed to be the right places. But no other hole matched the bolt holes in the girders to which they were fitted. He checked the code number stamped into them with that on the girder. It was correct.

One of the men stuck up an arm to indicate he was re-laying Jim's call, and a minute later Bart's arm flashed up in acknowledgment. The lead man rocketed over, landing with a practiced twist of the rocket tube that lined him up with the work. He stared at the plates, checked the code, and let out a call for Dan.

"Sabotage again," Bart reported, when the foreman arrived. "Dan, this can't go on. We're losing half the supplies."

"There were those beams yesterday . . ." Jim began. Then he stopped, staring down at the plates.

The beams hadn't fitted. And yet, on this shift, the man who was installing them had had no trouble with a lot of the same ones Jim had been unable to handle. The other man might have had more skill—but not that much more. There had to be some other explanation. Jim stared at the beams that were stacked off at the side, and down at those in place. Then he let out a shout that swung the two men to face him.

"It's the sunlight." He heard himself beginning to stammer as he forced the words out, took a breath, and went on more calmly. "Dan, I remember Dad had trouble on a bridge once when he couldn't get the two sides to line up at the end. One side was in the sunlight, the other in the shadow. And the heated side of the span had expanded. It's the same here."

He pointed it out, showing how the girders and beams in the piled supply dump were shielded from the Sun in places by the shadow of others, while those installed were receiving the full heat from the glaring sunlight.

"That's it!" Dan nodded. He found one of the plates

that had been warmed already, after coming out of the cooler interior of the rocket ship, and jerked it into alignment. The bolts went through easily.

The beams before had been forced into the slots left by the catchplates—and the upper side of the slot had been heated, while the lower was contracted in the shadow. Until the beams were in the same position for some time, they couldn't fit. Then those that had been stacked sidewise were still wrong.

"String out the parts the way they should be," Dan ordered. "And bolt them on with one bolt at a time until they warm up to match. We'll change our storing after this. Jim, this will go on your record; there's a bonus for smart ideas. I don't know how I missed it. Too many things, I guess. Space!"

Bart nodded his own approval. "I spent a year as a grunt on a line crew," he told Jim. "Half our work was figuring how much to allow for metal shrinkage in winter—and I never thought of it here. Neither did our engineer! Wait'll the college kids hear this."

"My father was a college man," Jim pointed out. "And he was the one who figured it out first. That's what education is for."

Bart laughed, turning to leave. "Sure, kid. I know it. But you don't have to tell them that, do you? Leave me a little fun in life."

The work went well enough after that. Once the metal was attached to other metal, convection of heat between the parts helped. Jim took time off to move out and turn all the beams lying alongside into the right position. Some had to be handled several times, since it was impossible to place them in position without any motion at all left. But when he began to run out of catchplates, he felt sure the beams would be ready.

He bolted the last plate down, feeling better than he had since he'd first learned that he was to go out into space. He unsnapped his belt, congratulating himself on having automatically fastened it without thinking about it. Then he stood up to go back for the beams.

His first awareness that he'd made a mistake came when he took the first step. His foot moved back, and his body jerked forward, but there was nothing under him! Ten feet way, the beam on which he'd stood seemed to be drifting off.

He'd reacted with Earth habits, just as he was congratulating himself that he'd overcome them. He'd tried to step, and the force of his effort had simply kicked him off into space, where he was sailing away from the work at several feet a second. He hadn't carried a line, counting on the belt. Now he was where he couldn't possibly reach for anything to get back.

For a second, panic hit him. If there had been another man near, someone could have thrown a rope. But he'd been too far.

Then he caught himself, and let out a yell for help. He waited for a reply. None came.

He'd been using his set a good deal, particularly during the ferrying with Jerry. He tried to remember the directions—something about checking his battery every shift. Had he checked it that morning? There'd been the visit to the nurse; he'd been held up while the other men filed out.

He hadn't checked it or replaced it for a fresh battery. It must have been growing weak for some time, and now had discharged below the level where it could trip the relay for speech!

He was cut off from the others—and rapidly leaving them behind for the empty, hungry depths of space.

Chapter 6 *Vertigo*

Jim fought his mind. His thoughts were racing off in a million frantic directions, but he pulled them back. There had to be an answer. He shut his eyes to cut out the sight of the distance that was separating him from everything else. He bit his teeth together, and clenched his fists inside the big space mittens. It must have happened to others. There was something that could be done.

Then he realized that there was still the space taxi. Jerry could take off in it and rescue him. He relaxed and began to breathe easier. The sweat was still running down from his forehead, threatening to blind him, but it began to dry as the worst of the fear left him.

He was swinging about slowly in an awkward end-over-end manner. He waited until he could spot the hut, and checked the position of the taxi.

It wasn't there!

While he swung about, he tried to spot it. Maybe Jerry was out on some other job—one where he could be called back. Maybe he was already on the way!

Then Jim saw the little taxi, lying beside the dump of material which was used as a machine shop for the repairing of their tools. Jerry was beside it. Jim swung over again, losing sight, but he strained to see as soon as he came around. Then he groaned.

Jerry had something lined up on a big block and was busy with that, while there was no tube sticking out behind the taxi as there should have been. The man was changing the lining of the rocket motor! He must be putting in a new nozzle! And it would mean that minutes—perhaps half an hour—would go by before he could get the taxi into operation.

The clicking of the breathing mechanism in Jim's suit reached his ears. He tried to estimate how much oxygen he had left, but his wrist watch was inside the suit where he couldn't see it, and he had no idea of time. He hadn't learned to count the revolutions around the Earth, allowing two hours for each. It might be the middle of the shift, or it might be near the end, where his oxygen supply would be running low.

He shouted again, knowing that no one could hear him, because his vocal cords had to let some of the tension out of him. He screamed, and caught himself. This was no time for hysteria. He'd seen men fall from a bridge construction job to their deaths because they panicked and went down thrashing about, instead of reaching out a steady hand for the cable or girder that was near.

He got control of himself again. When men were sent out on such a job, provision was always made for every emergency that could be predicted; a man was too valuable to waste, and Jim's society was one that placed the life of the individual first at all times.

Then he had it, and cursed himself for forgetting. There was the rocket tube hanging at his side. With that, he could blast out and force himself back.

Now suddenly he began to hope that no one would see him, and that he could get back on his own. He pulled out the tube with its heavy bulb at one end, its handgrip, and its tiny rocket nozzle at the other. There were printed instructions on the fuel bulb. He stared at them, the letters blurring in front of his eyes. He read enough to see how it was worked, and gave up on the rest. It was too hard to see against the glaring dazzle of the Sun—and in the shadow, the blackness was nearly complete with no air to diffuse light about.

He waited until he was facing away from the structure on which he'd been working, pointed the tube outward and pressed down on the little button.

It nearly tore his hand off. He'd set it for less than full force, but he'd underestimated the push it developed. He gripped it and fought against the pressure until it was back at his side. Then he cut it off to see what progress he was making.

Sickness clamped down on his stomach as he saw. The tube had bucked in his hand, moving out of the correct direction and going wild. Now he was spinning sideways and head over heels in a complicated motion that brought him face to face with the Sun once every second, and left it almost impossible to estimate his progress.

He forced himself to catch the swing of it, and to look only when he was facing the hut. It was coming toward him, but he was going to miss it by three hundred feet. He'd added speed away from the spot he'd left, instead of counteracting it.

He tried to get a line on his direction. This time he put the rocket tube against his stomach and held it firmly, before firing it as he came to the right spot.

It kicked back on him, like a mule, and he doubled over with agony. The tube went wild again for a few seconds, before its fuel was completely exhausted.

By sheer chance, it had nearly counteracted his sideways spin. He was still moving end over end, but more slowly. For a second, he began to hope as he seemed to be making progress toward the hut. Then he groaned. He'd slowed himself down somewhat, and had set his course closer to the hut. But he still was going to miss it by at least fifty feet more than the length of the cord he had tied to him. Even if someone got there in time, he didn't have a chance.

Vainly, he tried to squeeze another blast out of the rocket tube, but it was empty. His eyes fell on the printing he hadn't read, and he grunted. It was a warning to set the valve to the red dot and to use it only at low power for short bursts until the user could familiarize himself with its effect. He'd let himself be panicked into overlooking the simplest precautions.

He laughed bitterly at himself. He'd done everything wrong. He had no one to blame except himself. He'd always been able to take care of things by himself, and he hadn't had sense enough to know when he couldn't.

The self-denunciation helped to clear his thinking, somehow. Now he could see that the men at work on the station were all watching him. Apparently the rocket blast had called their attention to him, at least.

They were strung out, a long way from the hut. Two of them were busy tying cords about their middles and adding other cords to it. He saw them lift their rocket tubes. They were going to try to come after him.

He breathed more easily, beginning a prayer of thanks. Then someone else ran over to them, pointing toward Jim and the hut with short, choppy gestures. The two men stopped and stared. For a time, they seemed to hesitate. Then they began taking off the cords and going back to work.

Jim was trembling with reaction from the hope he'd had. They could at least have tried! There would have been no harm in that, since they would have had the cords to pull themselves back. Maybe they couldn't have reached him, but they could have tried! The blood rang in his ears, and he could hear the ticking of his breathing apparatus. It sounded slower to him, and there was a stuffy quality to the air. It might have been his imagination, but he couldn't be sure.

Then he became aware of a faint buzzing in his ear. He shook his head, as he made out one of the figures who might have been either Dan or Bart—probably Dan from his size—waving toward him. He realized suddenly that the buzzing must be his earphones working; no relay was needed to receive. He tried to listen, but the batteries were wearing out too fast, and he only got a few faint hisses.

He tried to make sense of the waving arms of the man who was trying to signal him. The man seemed to be trying to wave toward him and the hut.

Did they think he should swim over to the hut? Didn't they know that his rocket tube was exhausted?

He shook his head. The man waving stopped, shrugged, and nodded emphatically, making a curving motion toward the hut with his arm.

The other men were back at work. If they were watching him, there was no way to see.

Jim estimated his distances again, this time coldly and

clearly. He found a point on the end of the girders and used that to sight himself against the hut. He would come a little closer than he had thought, but he was going to miss it by too far for any chance of rescue if they were afraid to take chances with their rocket tubes.

It hurt. Somehow, he could have taken it if they had made any effort to save him. It was like the men in the garage when he was fired. They could have said that it was tough luck and wished him better luck elsewhere. It had been the same at the aircraft plant. He'd gotten along all right with everyone, but nobody had been close to him. He'd been too busy at his work to stop for the horseplay that went on among the others. He'd been so busy trying to make good that he hadn't even learned the names of most of them.

But they'd have tried to save him, if he'd been in trouble like this. He was sure of that. What kind of men did it take to work in space—men who had no emotions? He couldn't believe it, knowing Dan and remembering what he could of Bart.

For long minutes, his emotions caught him. His stomach was heaving with the strain, and the emptiness of space pressed in harder and harder. The feeling of having nothing under him came back. He could feel himself falling. His eyes centered on the Earth, a thousand miles away, and he could feel himself falling every foot of the way.

He was sick abruptly. He had barely time to duck his head so that he missed the inside of his helmet. His stomach heaved and tears of shock ran from his eyes.

That sobered him. The vertigo passed, and he went through a period of reaction where the idea of dying no longer seemed so horrible. It wouldn't be too bad—there'd be no pain. He'd simply pass out from lack of air.

Then he shook it off, and began thinking again; for the first time since he'd lost his footing, his mind was clear and cold.

For every action there is an equal and opposite reaction. If he could throw anything to his left, his body would drift to the right. He had the rope, the empty rocket tube, and his hammer! Together, they probably had a mass of one-fortieth as much as he had. He could throw them with force great enough to give them a speed of at least forty miles an hour—a good pitcher could double that, at least—and that should change his direction of drift by a side thrust of at least one mile an hour—a foot and a half a second!

But it had to be soon, before he passed the hut! Maybe that was what the man signaling him had meant. Jim groped for the hammer, and took careful aim.

Then he shoved it back in amazement. He was moving toward the hut in a direction that would bring him much closer than he had thought! He'd pass it within the length of a normal rope. And standing on the hut near where he'd pass was a figure in a space suit, waiting for him.

He puzzled over it. Once a body was given motion in any direction, it tried to stay in that direction in a straight line, unless acted on by some outside force. The station tried to go in a straight line, and the gravity of the Earth bent it into a circle. But what had changed his direction here where there was no such outside force?

He puzzled over it, while watching the figure with the rope get ready for him, and the answer was obvious, once he realized it. Everything in the universe has some gravity attached to it—but for anything smaller that a planet, that is a very tiny force. Small as it was, however, the pull of the station hut on him had been great enough to change his direction slightly. It had had a great deal of time to keep pulling with that faint, weak force of its gravity, and it had been enough. The men hadn't deserted him. They had known, and had tried to make him understand.

Then he was near the hut, and the rope came sailing out with a heavy weight at its end. It sailed out in front of where he would pass, with two feet to spare, and stayed there, as if it were a rigid rod. He put out a hand carefully, and caught it.

A minute later he was being dragged back toward the hut. The figure there was braced against the handholds, taking up the strain of hauling him in. He made no effort to pull himself down, knowing that it would only increase the pull on the other.

Then the hut was beside him. His hand went out for a hold and clung to it, while the aching breath caught in his throat and he panted, hanging on desperately. The space-suited figure tried to lift Jim. He bent and made an effort to help, but his muscles were too weak. He felt himself lifted and dragged along until they were through the air lock and going down the hall toward the nurse's office.

The space suit fell off the other, revealing the nurse herself as the one who had saved him. She began stripping off his space suit, then stopped and led him toward the bathroom.

"Can you take care of yourself?" she asked. "I don't mind helping, but if you'd rather . . ."

"I'll do it, please," he begged. He swallowed thickly, and tried to smile his gratitude. "And thanks! I—I . . ."

She smiled back, and there was more warmth in it than in most professional smiles he had seen. "It wasn't anything, Jim. I happened to be the one to take the call when it came in here, so I went out. Take it easy, and yell if you need any help. When you're finished, come into my office."

He rolled the space suit and his underclothes into a matted ball and shoved them inside the plastic bag in which he kept the space suit. Then he was climbing into the welcome bath bag, feeling the reviving touch of the clean water. He was still shaking, half with reaction and half with a memory of how he must have looked to her.

When he finished, he tried to wash his clothes. But the nurse knocked and shoved the partition aside a crack to throw in his other clothes. "Leave those," she told him. "I'll take care of them. And I want you in here for an inspection."

He hated the idea, but he did as he was told. Dan was standing at the door of her office as he came through. The foreman looked at him apologetically. "Jim, I tried to tell you . . . I thought you got it. If I'd known your battery was shot, I'd have come out to you myself."

"Mr. Bailey, you'll have to leave," Nora cut in quickly.

"You can explain all that later. Jim, get up here on this table and strap down. I'm going to go over you with the massager while I check up on you. There, now. Nice and gentle. Just relax, Jim. Isn't that soothing? You can go to sleep if you want to. Sleep."

He felt the soft, regular motion of the massager. It soothed him and he pretended to sleep to humor her, while she checked on his heart and blood pressure again and gave him a shot of something.

He was almost asleep when he heard Bart talking to Nora. Jim felt himself lifted before he could open his eyes and carried gently along, then placed on his sleeping wall and strapped down. He tried to say something, but Bart held a hand against his lips.

"Shh, Jim. You go on back to sleep. We can talk tomorrow."

Jim let himself relax until the big man left again. But the sleep wouldn't come now. He'd made a complete fool of himself this time. When they gave him his walking papers back to Earth, he'd make no protests. But it would hurt. He'd begun to like space, before this happened. And in spite of the horror and sick vertigo of the last hour, he still liked it.

Chapter 7 *Paint Job*

The hardest thing Jim had ever done was to start for breakfast at the beginning of the next shift. He had found his clothes and space suit neatly laid out beside him, and had put them on. Now he headed down the hall. Let them say what they would, he wouldn't hide like a scared dog in a corner.

Nora called out from her office, and he turned, expecting another examination. Instead, she floated over beside him. "How do you feel, Jim?"

"Grateful. Foolish. And otherwise fine," he reported.

She smiled casually. "You should feel foolish, worrying about it. Everybody here has been in some trouble, sooner or later. I tried to go out of the air lock without a space suit the second day—almost got out before Mr. Bailey saw me. Bart Smith jumped after a wrench that got away and they had to send for him in the taxi. Nobody thinks anything of it—except that you've passed!"

"Passed? Why, because I got in a mess you had to help me out of?"

"Stop it!" She frowned at him, then shrugged. "No. But you were in pretty normal physical condition afterward, and you didn't crack up. Now you're wearing your space suit, as if you don't mind going out again. After an experience like that, men either crack completely or else they adapt to space. Mr. Bailey and Bart were betting you'd be wearing your suit."

He puzzled over it, wondering what else he could have worn. Even if they had shipped him back, he'd have needed the space suit to get to the rocket. If they let him stay, he'd need it for work. Then he remembered the man who'd been carried into the air lock screaming; probably that one hadn't wanted to be put into a space suit again.

Bart looked up as he sat down at the table beside Nora. "Hi, kid. Feel up to some rigging today?"

"You're the lead man," Jim answered, and heard a sigh go up from the other men. Conversation picked up normally, with no one mentioning the trouble of the day before.

He could feel them watching him tautly as he headed for the air lock on the way out to work. For a second, his stomach felt queasy, and the cold emptiness of space nagged at a corner of his mind. Then he began checking his battery and examining his belt for cracks, and the feeling passed. He filed out with the others, while Dan beamed at him. The foreman caught his arm as he started out along the ropes toward the end of the extension. "That's for new men, Jim. Feel up to coming along with me?"

Jim followed the motion of his hand across the open space toward the job. He hesitated for a second. "If you think I can, it's okay with me, Dan."

"Good boy!" The foreman bent his knees and took off across the emptiness.

Jim swallowed once, sighted the way carefully, and leaped after him. For a second, the falling feeling hit at him again. Then he was floating along easily without effort, at a better speed than he could have walked on Earth. He checked his course, saw he was going to land within a few feet of where he'd aimed, and stretched out a careful hand to check his speed at the end.

As he stood up, he knew one answer to the questions he had. He might succeed in passing into space, or he might have to go back to Earth forever after this job. He might get killed while working here. But he was a spaceman now, and he had a job to do. Even if he couldn't stay in space, he could make sure that someone would.

The work went on more easily in the following days. New men came up from Earth, and most of them went back. One of them did almost the same thing Jim had done, but turned his rocket tube on while it was still pointing toward his helmet. Nobody got much work done that day, and there was no conversation at dinner. But the next day, another man passed the three-day time limit without trouble, and they went back to work. Down on Earth, the tests became surer, and more of those sent up stayed with them.

Dan had to do most of the work. Thorndyke stayed in his office or came out for quick inspections while at the station. But the engineer's big job was to keep things moving, and he had learned to trust Dan. He made regular trips back to Earth, changing orders and specifications as they found it necessary. Every third trip, Mark came up and would often talk to Jim.

On Earth, things were coasting along as always. But there was a growing undercurrent in the tissue-thin news-paper that came up with each rocket. The Combine was restless, as if it knew something was going on in America. The World Congress was bogged down in details of where the next meeting should be. The men on it were good men, who tried hard, but they were whipped as long as even one of the major governments didn't want them to succeed.

Jim read the letters to the editor, and was surprised at the number who wrote in hopelessly, angrily or bitterly to demand why nothing was being done about building a space station. The paper shipped to the men was a cautious, reliable one which had never gone in for the hysteria of some of the others, but the readers were worried. One of the new hydrogen bombs could wipe out all of New York. Fifty could cripple the country hopelessly. And the only defense that seemed reliable was to have a superior force of bombs in a station in the sky to prevent aggression.

Jim remembered his own belief in that. But now he wondered how many of them had any idea of the difficulty of building such a station. It had taken years of planning and work to get the method of construction developed to a practical point. Dan indicated that the men who'd first come up with him had doubted whether they could get it started at all.

When an India-paper set of magazines came up, Jim turned to the science fiction ones first. There were no stories about space stations now. The writers seemed to have decided that it was hopeless, something that would never be done. They were writing about new atomic drives that permitted a rocket to take off from Earth and go straight to the Moon, or about domes of force that could make a nation safe from bombs. But under the hope of their stories was a bitter pessimism that had never been part of science fiction as a whole before.

It seemed wrong not to tell the people. There must be some way in which it could be handled. But Jim had to admit that he was no expert on political affairs, and that men who knew more might have good reasons for what they did. It was his business to help get the station up and finished, so the men below could announce the secret.

He wondered if they would announce it, however. They hadn't been able to conceal the atom bomb. But there had been endless work that might have benefited humanity since then, locked up in restricted drawers, where it could benefit only the few. No wonder the world was growing bitter.

Yet, curiously, there was still hope. It showed in the fact that they wrote those letters about the space station. They had learned to think of getting beyond Earth, and to believe that a better world could be made. That was progress beyond what had been true a hundred years before.

Nora had been discussing it with him when Dan came up behind them and caught the tail end of it. The foreman sighed. "You kids take things too seriously," he said automatically. Then his own voice betrayed him with its worry. "I just hope they let us get the station up. Once war is declared, this will come to an end."

"It can't!" Jim cried hotly.

"It can and will, boy. Don't think the Combine doesn't know about Johnston Island, whether they know of us or not. We've been having fleet exercises there for three years —in the waters around. That's enough to tip them off. And one bit of evidence can be added to another. Maybe they've tracked our rockets on their radar. They'd think of the rockets as war weapons, and the first place to get an atomic bomb would be the Island."

"But what about us?" Nora asked.

The lines in Dan's face deepened. "I wish I knew, Nora. I wish I did. I guess we'd just have to wait here—as long as we could last."

They wouldn't have had to wait at all if the next day one of the new cooks hadn't eaten the pie made from dried peaches, before the men had a chance at it. They'd finally gotten a doctor by then to take the strain off Nora, and he tested the pie after pumping out the cook's stomach futilely. "Botulism," he announced grimly. *"Bacillus botulinus.* And that makes no sense, because the poison from the stuff is destroyed in five minutes of cooking. It had to be put in after the pie was baked."

They tried to find who could have put the poisonous germs into the food, but there was no way of knowing. The cooks had little room in the kitchen, and had slipped the sealed tins out into the common hall to cool before giving the men a special treat. Anyone could have done it, but it must have required a good supply of the deadly stuff. It was a grim place for a few days after that, as useless checks were made on everyone. But every man in the place had already been triply checked by Earth.

"Sabotage." Dan said tensely. "All we can do is watch! We've got a spy. Now let's make sure he can't report back. And don't forget that the man who can pass all the security checks won't be someone we can spot here just because we don't like him."

Yet the work went on. They finished the framing girders around the wheel, and more men came up and swarmed along them. There were plumbers for the miles and miles of pipework needed. Electricians laid down their lines. Carpenters worked on the light sound-deadening board that was to serve as partitions. The place became a swarm, and the hut had to be extended. Now Bart was a foreman, as were several others, and Dan was working directly under the two engineers who had come out to join Thorndyke.

They had begun putting the metal sheathing around the whole wheel. That would serve eventually as a meteor bumper, with a heavy fabric held inside it to form the inner wall. With that, they were frantically trying to get up the big solar mirror that would give them power enough to operate the station efficiently. The generators and turbines were coming up on the rockets, and trained men were working on the assembly and placement of them. Once the walls of the station were up, it was easier for men to stand life up here.

Jim was on the constant jump. Sometimes he suspected that Bart assigned the worst jobs to him deliberately. But it didn't matter. While it made it tougher on him, it also gave him a chance to learn more than most of the others. He'd lost four pounds, but he didn't miss them up here.

He wasn't surprised when he was assigned to the job of helping paint the solar mirror. This was a big trough that was to run all around the top of the station, set to face the Sun. It was curved to focus the rays of the Sun on a blackened pipe that ran down its center. In the pipe, mercury would be heated into a gas, at a temperature of thirteen hundred degrees Fahrenheit. This would drive a highly efficient "steam" turbine, which would drive a generator for the needed power. When all its energy was used, the mercury would be returned to the outside, to cool in the shadow of the mirror, condensing back to a liquid before re-use.

It was valuable work, and the station badly needed a good supply of power. But painting the mirror was done with liquid sodium. It was a silvery metal that melted easily at a low temperature. On Earth, it was so violently corrosive that it could snatch oxygen out of water. But in a vacuum, it made an excellent reflective paint. The only trouble was that it had to be handled with extreme caution.

Jim worked like a beaver trying to build a dam all alone, but he couldn't keep up with the men who were laying the trough and piping. Dan appointed a second man to the job. And then a third was chosen.

It was nasty work. A drop on the plasticized fabric of the space suits would burn a hole through them almost at once. Or a few drops left carelessly on the special gloves they wore for the job could explode violently if carried into the hut, to spread damage and dangerous wounds everywhere nearby.

Jim worked on cautiously, blending his speed with safety in a hard-earned lesson. But the first hour after the new man came out was enough to drive his nerves to the ragged edge. At first, the man began by painting the blackened pipe inside the trough.

Jim explained patiently that the pipe was blackened to absorb heat, and that the silver coating ruined it. He had to go back and construct a seat over the trough on which he could sit without touching the sodium, and then had to remove the metal chemically.

Finally, he gave up. The man was one of those whose intelligence was fine, but who never used it except for purely theoretical problems. He was either so bemused by space or so wrapped up in some inner excitement over being there that he didn't think—he followed orders blindly. Here no orders could cover everything. They were already slightly behind their schedule.

"All right," he said finally. "Go back to Dan and tell him Terrence and I can do it alone. Put your paint in the shop, and mark it dangerous. I'll clean up when I come in."

He watched the man leave, and turned to the boy who had been working with him. "Think we can do it, Terrence?"

"If God hadn't meant me to do the work, Jim, he'd never have let me pass the tests to get here, in spite of the prayers I said." Terrence Rodriguez was no heavier than a hundred pounds, soaking wet, but he had never complained, and his work was always all that Jim could ask. He'd spent his childhood doing hard work to help a family of seven younger children, and he was used to doing his utmost. "I'll race you."

"No—just keep up," Jim advised. Racing was a good way to get more work done—but also a fine way to invite carelessness.

They swung on, unconsciously switching sides to avoid overheating one side. Behind them, the metal gleamed like a mirror. Ahead, a gang of seven men were busy setting up the trough, while others worked on the elaborate plumbing.

Then suddenly Terrence dropped his brush into the sodium and pointed, his mouth open and working silently.

Jim swung about to see what was causing it, and his own mouth jerked open soundlessly.

The roof of the hut ahead of them was glowing hotly, and as they watched, it suddenly began crumbling away, while a great gout of flame rushed out as the air escaped. Oxygen and heat were fatal to the magnesium alloy out of which the plates were made.

"Down!" Jim ordered. He capped his can automatically, not bothering to pull the brush out. He began scrambling down, with Terrence at his heels. They dashed into the open section that had been left for a workshop, putting their cans carefully into a safety tank. Then they swung toward the old air lock.

The fire had been coming from the second air lock, installed when the hut was extended. The old one still worked, and men were inside the hut, laboring in space suits. An automatic door had snapped shut between the two sections at the first break in the airtight outer sheathing. But there were still men inside where the flames were, and they were being dragged out of a small emergency lock between the two sections.

One of them yanked off his helmet to cough harshly. His face was burned, but he seemed unaware of it. "Kid came through the lock with a can of something. He tripped, spilled it all over—and then it exploded. We tried to stop it, but it got away. The kid—"

He shuddered, and Jim found that his own body was suddenly weak and shaky. The third man must have done it. He'd taken the orders too literally—he'd gone to report to Dan first, before putting away the sodium. A solid hour's lecture on the dangers of the stuff had meant nothing to him.

Then Jim frowned. It seemed impossible that he could have made a mistake. Yet he couldn't believe that a saboteur would willingly sacrifice his own life to wipe out the station. He'd heard of it, but . . .

He dropped it to go in with Bart and Dan to survey the hopeless wreck that had been the hut extension.

Chapter 8 Foul Weather Below

The new section that had been added so recently was a total wreck. Everything in it seemed to have been destroyed, and the miracle was that no one but the man responsible had been killed. The flames had spread through it at a savage rate; but then the hole had broken through the outer layer, and the air had gone rushing out. Its disappearance into space had stopped the spread backward from the big oxygen supply that had still kept feeding it as the oxygen rushed for the hole—and left the rear of the extension almost airless.

The heat had been terrific, but, for the short time it had taken to get the men out, the space suits had protected them.

Tools, equipment, and all the things needed to protect the men from space and keep them alive had been wrecked.

"We'll have to double up in the remaining space until we can rebuild," Dan said wearily. "Jim, he was with you, wasn't he?"

Jim nodded, and told what he could. The foreman nodded in turn, his face without emotion. "Okay, it wasn't your fault, because nobody can foresee the behavior of a fool. I don't think it was sabotage. I wish I could; then we'd be free of our spy. But that's just the type of nonsense I've seen time and again on the best-run construction jobs."

There was nothing they could do for the moment but abandon the extension. The original hut still stood, and behind it lay another extension. Between the two, they could exist for a while, though it wouldn't be comfortable.

"Check the oxygen supplies first," the voice of Thorndyke, the head engineer, suggested.

Bart and Dan went off to do that, and Jim followed behind them. But from their faces, he could tell that their hopes weren't too high. Obviously, most of the oxygen had been put into the new extension, since there was more room there for the big containers of liquid oxygen. They had been in the shadow, below the main part of the hull, where they could stay liquid; but the heat of the fire had bent and twisted them, and some had even exploded violently.

"Takes three pounds of oxygen a day for a man," Dan said. "You'll find the amount on the outside of the tanks. Gauge will tell you what per cent has been used." He went back into the rear extension, leaving Bart and Jim to count the amount in the original hut. It was a lot less than they would have liked.

Dan came back with his figures, and they reported to Thorndyke. The engineer thought it over, checking his charts. "Umm. It checks. I was hoping there'd be an error in my lists. None stored outside?"

"Twenty tanks for use in the welders," Dan said, "or about that. We've run low because the supply rocket is due with more oxygen today."

Thorndyke's mouth twitched faintly. "There'll be a little delay on that, I'm afraid. I got word on the radar that they had canceled the shipment for today."

"They'd better get it up," Bart said flatly. "According to those figures, we've got just enough air left for all the men here for about thirty hours! And we don't have chemicals to soak up the carbon dioxide they breathe out for even that long."

Nora had come out and heard the last. She caught at Jim's sleeve, and her eyes grew round and frightened. But she said nothing. The engineer nodded, and motioned them back to his quarters.

Jim had never been there before, and even the danger that was pressing in on them couldn't completely deaden his curiosity. He stared at the blue-print table, the files of other prints, the drafting supplies, and all the scientific books on the closed shelves. His father had been one of the older type of engineers, who had depended almost entirely on a few basic books, a slide rule, and what he could carry in his head; he'd also worked closely with his men, more like Dan than like Thorndyke. Yet Jim realized that his father couldn't have guided the building of this station according to the enormous complexity of the charts. Thorndyke obviously could, with the help of such men as Dan.

The engineer opened a closet on the ceiling and pulled out a radar transmitter on a slide. He belted himself down in front of it and began pounding on a key attached. Jim could read enough Morse code to know that it was an SOS, but the rest of it was beyond him.

"I just hope no spy picks up the direction this comes from," Thorndyke said, without interrupting his sending. "As it is, I'm going to be in trouble for sending when we're not directly over our pickup station. But this is emergency enough to justify it, I guess. Ah!"

He'd stopped a few seconds before. Now an answer began coming in from the huge transmitter on Earth. The answer was in voice, instead of code, since Jim could hear sounds like speech from the earphones.

"Ouch!" Thorndyke put the phones down and turned to the others. "They say they can't send a ship up now. Johnston Island is in the middle of a storm with a high wind. They've got the big sticks—the rockets, that is—tied down, but it isn't safe to use them."

He shook his head. "Any of you know anything about that? I'm no expert on rockets. I think what they say makes sense, but if it doesn't, I want to blast them off their fat seats and get them moving!"

"It makes sense," Jim said reluctantly. "I had two years of rocketry at Central Tech, and we got through that much. You can't take off in a high wind. The first few seconds, the rocket just barely rises—and it has poor control at best. The trajectory up out of the atmosphere has to be pretty carefully figured, or all future figures will go wrong. If the wind tips it—even if it doesn't fall over—it will be off course beyond the ability of the automatic pilot to handle."

"That's about what I thought." Thorndyke tapped his pencil against his teeth, considering. "What do you think, Dan?"

Dan's wide face was disgusted. "You're talking theory,

and you're listening to the guy at the transmitter there spouting it at you from Earth. Why not get in touch with one of the pilots? They're the boys who know what can be done."

"Good point." Thorndyke turned back to his transmitter, and the key pounded busily again. He waited. There was a short answer. "He's calling the pilots." Then there was silence for a long time.

The four of them crowded around, trying to get close enough to the headphone Thorndyke held out to hear. The voice came through thinly, weakened by having to travel from the phone through a foot or so of distance. But they could just make out the words.

"This is Gantry. If it's the emergency you birds claim it is, we'll have to risk it. I figure there's a fifty-fifty chance. We've drawn lots, and I'll be coming to pay you a visit as soon as I can get loaded. But don't count too much on my getting through. Do what you can up your way."

The phone went dead. Jim sighed softly, knowing that he had heard a man who expected to be dead within hours —and the others in the room had recognized the same tone. "If he'd thought he had one chance in ten, he'd have said it was a cinch," Bart said. "If any of you guys know how to pray, you'd better start doing so."

There was no sense in trying to keep the facts from the men. If they had been the sort who needed comfort in a time of trouble, they wouldn't have been in the station. Dan and Thorndyke put it to the whole crew, without sparing any details.

"We've got about fifteen hours' supply of chemicals to soak up the carbon dioxide we exhale," Thorndyke summed it up. "After that, things will get muggy in here, but we may have an extra few hours to go if we let some of the oxygen and dioxide leak out into space, replacing it with fresh oxygen from the tanks. That wastes the gas— but it gets rid of some of the wastes, too. Still, we either get new supplies in less than twenty hours, or we can forget them."

"How about the storm? Is it going to let up?" one of the men yelled from the back.

Thorndyke moved to the lock, pulling on his helmet, and the men followed him. They crowded out slowly, holding onto the handholds and girders around, while the engineer pointed down to the Earth spinning below. "Take a look," he said.

Jim had stopped looking at the world below him. Without a telescope, not much could be seen. Clouds and haze kept a partial cover over it, and only at rare intervals could the outline of a continent be seen. There were gaps where the ground or water showed through, but without magnification they were meaningless.

Now, as the engineer pointed out the location of Johnston Island to them, they began studying the great ball. They were on the sunward side, and it was easy to perceive that a whole section over the Pacific was a solid blanket of clouded obscurity.

"All that you see is part of the storm. It's circling over that area, and heading east. The Island isn't going to hit the storm center, as you can see. If it did, they'd have a little time in which things would be quiet, before the wind swung the other way. But the best guess I can make from what they tell me is that it's going to take about thirty-six hours before they're out of it. Someday, after this is finished and when we get good meteorologists up here where they can see all that goes on down there, we'll be able to predict the weather exactly. Now, all they can do is to guess."

They filed back inside, taking it easy under Dan's orders to avoid burning up any more oxygen than they had to. Eating was cut down. Whether it would speed up oxygen consumption or not, nobody seemed to know for sure, but there was no harm in trying.

Jim was lucky. He was kept busy bringing in the tanks from the welders and the few small reserves that would normally have been kept in various locations for an emergency, if a tank on a suit needed quick replacement. Valves sometimes stuck, and it was handy to have spares. But the total didn't amount to much.

Surprisingly, there wasn't as much fear and gloom as Jim had expected. It was as if everyone there had stopped thinking of the station as a small island in the great sea of space; bit by bit, they had begun to think of it as a world, and it was inconceivable that it could come to an end.

He wasn't kidding himself that way. He was scared, whenever he had time to think, and he could see that Dan and Thorndyke were also scared.

Thorndyke stayed at the radar set, until he got word that the take-off was about due. They were always approximately within viewing range of a rocket at take-off, since the rocket had to parallel their course in getting itself up. The ship took fifty-six minutes to swing halfway around the world on its upward hop, and the station took an hour to cover the same distance in its orbit. But it was close enough—except that no rocket could be seen from a thousand miles above.

But it was night over Johnston Island now, and they hoped to see a faint flash as it broke through the clouds. Jim and several others were outside the hut in their suits, staring down at the darkened side of the globe below them. It presented a crescent now, like the half-moon, with the Island just beyond the edge of the darkness.

Dan relayed the information from the radar to them, through the tiny set in his helmet. "They've taken off. Gantry kicked out his radarman and is going it with just the copilot."

"There!" It was a spontaneous shout from several voices in the phones. Jim strained his eyes, and could just see a faint, weak trail where the exhaust of the great first stage must be spreading through the blanket of clouds. It looked wrong to him somehow—as if it were headed straight up. But he couldn't be sure. He had to blink his eyes every other second to keep from missing it altogether.

Nobody seemed to be breathing. The faint trace was gone now, as if the rocket had risen above the clouds, and was too weak to be seen by itself.

"They report he had rough going on the way up, but straightened at the last minute. He's planning on wasting

72

fuel for manual correction, even if he doesn't have enough for the return leg," Dan's voice reported. "Looks like he may make it!"

They waited for seconds, with nothing to see. By now, Jim knew, the first stage should have been kicked free. But it would be too tiny a burst to show up.

Then a groan went up. Jim blinked again, and caught it. Far from the spot where the first blast of light had shown, there was a larger, hotter spot. It mushroomed out to a visible circle, and then began fading slowly.

"What is it?" Terrence's voice sounded in Jim's ears.

He shook his head, unwilling to say what he suspected. His voice seemed to be stuck in his throat.

"What happened?" Dan asked harshly.

Jim took another look, but there was nothing to be seen now. "I think we've had it—and so has he," he reported. "There was a flash of light too bright for anything except an explosion. He must have been pretty badly knocked around on the way up. Something may have happened to the first stage. I'm only guessing, but it looked as if his first stage wouldn't break free, and he finally had to risk blowing it clear with the rockets from the second stage."

Jim had seen speculations on whether that could be done in some of the more fanciful books he had read. And in an emergency, there was nothing else a pilot could do. Without being able to free the first stage, he was inevitably bound to drop back to the Earth.

"I guess it didn't work," he said slowly. "The pressure blew the explosion back into the tanks, and they caught."

He turned to go back, but Thorndyke was coming out, staring down at the world where nothing showed. He touched helmets with Jim. "What about the pilot? Could he get free?"

"Maybe, sir—if the final stage didn't get caught in the explosion. He has an ejector and parachute built onto the seat, and the suit would protect him, if he could get it on."

He hadn't realized that everyone could hear, since he'd forgotten to turn the radio off. Behind him, there was a sigh. One of the men bent forward further, to stare at the world where their rescue had failed.

"God have mercy on his soul," a voice said, and there was a chorus of "Amen" from the others.

"And on us, too," Nora said softly.

Only silence answered that as they stared from one to another.

Chapter 9 The Stolen Papers

There were about twenty at the council of war in Thorndyke's cabin. They sat about the room, perched on the furniture, some suspended from one wall, some from others. It brought their heads closer together than would have been possible in any gathering of the same size on Earth, and they'd stopped thinking that a man looked odd when upside down.

"The big problem's in getting rid of the carbon dioxide," Thorndyke said flatly. "If we could handle that, we might just barely survive until the storm had let up enough for another ship to try. I've been in touch with Earth. Mark Emmett has volunteered to try it right now, but has been refused. I advised them to refuse. It won't do the project any good to lose another ship. They can lose us and start over—but they can't lose the rocket."

There were grunts at that, but no objections. Jim had thought of Thorndyke as some outsider, but now he realized that the engineer was one of them—a man who had dreamed of a station here until it meant more than anything else could mean.

"Do we have to get rid of it?" one of the other engineers asked. "It isn't a poison, but carbon monoxide is. That's the one which kills people, but I've heard that carbon dioxide is safe enough."

They all turned to Dr. Perez. He was almost forty, and the oldest man there. After they had sent up three other doctors who couldn't stand space, he had volunteered from the testing unit at the Island, and had surprised everyone by passing with flying colors. In the station, he'd had a rough time of it the first three days, but now he seemed quite at home among them.

"I'm not an expert on that," he qualified his answer. "But no, carbon dioxide isn't a poison, exactly. However, the presence of excessive carbon dioxide in the air will make the heart beat faster and the lungs speed up. The body thinks there is too much in the lungs or system, instead of outside, and tries to get rid of it. When the concentration is too high, it becomes very hard for the lungs to extract it from the blood—it reaches a balance, that is. And when it can't be extracted, the body can die in its own waste. We can probably stand a pretty high concentration, though. Before we start spilling air out into space, we'd better let it get uncomfortable, at least."

"Anybody here know enough chemistry to help?" Thorndyke asked.

A young man in the background nodded. "That's why I came to you. But now I can't help. Mr. Bailey says we don't have any of the things I've suggested."

In a vague way, Jim still felt responsible for the trouble. He should have checked on his assistant. He'd been beating his head, trying to remember what he'd learned in high school about the behavior of the gas. His father had always maintained that a man could accomplish almost anything by reducing things down to the basic characteristics, and then finding out what was done in other fields.

"It's a heavy gas," someone said suddenly. "If we all climb up to the top where the lighter oxygen is . . ."

He realized his mistake before the others swung on him. Thorndyke chuckled grimly. "It's the same here as anything else—neither light nor heavy," he pointed out. "But all the same, you're moving in the right direction. What are the basic characteristics of carbon dioxide?"

The young man who'd studied chemistry piped up again. "It's a heavy gas, composed of one atom of carbon and two of oxygen. Animals breathe it out, and plants breathe it in, releasing the oxygen again. It freezes directly to a solid, without any real liquid state, and is then known as dry ice. It evaporates . . ."

"It freezes at a higher temperature than air!" Jim shouted. "That's how they make dry ice—they lower the temperature enough for carbon dioxide to freeze, but the rest of the atmosphere stays a gas. What about the cold side —does it get cold enough to freeze it out?"

"How cold?" Thorndyke asked. "Never mind." He reached over for a copy of the *Handbook of Chemistry and Physics* and ran through it. "If we didn't pass it through too fast, our air would probably lose most of the gas from the cold. Dan, any way to get a gastight pan . . ."

"You've got the pipes under the solar mirror trough," Dan pointed out. "They're all coupled up. We could blow it through there slowly enough—trial and error should tell us how slowly."

They broke up. The men who had been handling the plumbing were gone first, grabbing for their space suits as they discussed ways of breaking into the cooling piping and coupling it to the airtight part of the hut. Originally, it had led to the section of the station where the power plant was being installed.

There were parts enough for the change-over, and the air pumps used to evacuate the air locks would do as compressors to drive air through the pipes.

"Eventually the pipes would clog up with the stuff," Dan admitted to Thorndyke. "But for the few hours left after our chemicals run out, they should handle it. And we can always thaw it out afterward by leaving a section open to space and running a little heater along it."

"Why wait to have the chemicals break down?" Jim asked. "Why not use it as soon as we can? It'll put less load on the tubes."

Thorndyke nodded quick approval.

Some hope revived among the men as they saw something being done. Jim went with Thorndyke and Dan to study the storm center over the Pacific when it came into view under them again. Quite a few hours had already gone by, and there was some visible change. But it still looked as if they would be out of oxygen before they could get help from below. It all depended on how much less than three pounds of oxygen a man could breathe in twenty-four hours and still live.

They came back inside to find Dr. Perez busy injecting

77

some of the men. "Putting them to sleep," the doctor explained. "They use less oxygen when they're sleeping. Some have gone off by themselves, claiming they can sleep without drugs."

Jim turned toward his own sleeping compartment, but Thorndyke pulled him back. "No sleep for you!"

Jim waited, but the man made no explanation. He stirred uncomfortably. "All right, sir. But you'll have to tell me what I'm supposed to do."

"You're supposed to think!" Thorndyke said. He swung an arm around the hut. "That's what all men are supposed to do, Jim—but some do it more than others. You've been doing all right so far. Maybe you won't have any more ideas—maybe none of us will—but I feel better knowing the men who've contributed are awake. And stop worrying about the fact that you didn't nurse your helper every step of the way back!"

"Yes, sir," Jim agreed. But it wasn't that easy. He didn't really feel guilty, but the fact remained that he could have saved all the trouble if he'd been able to think far enough ahead.

He had no more ideas. The plumbers came back to report that the pipes had been recoupled to the hut now, and the electricians and helpers began tearing out the blowers and reinstalling them. The air was soon circulating through the pipes. They had no way to tell whether it was working, except by an examination of the contents of those pipes. Periodically, they stopped the blowers and ran a fine wire up them, pulling it back and looking for crystals of dry ice. When there were none, they cut the amount of air going through them.

Eventually, the welcome sight of the tiny crystals rewarded them, and they left the setting. The air was cold now, though much less cold than had been expected. Most of the men were asleep, but the rest went around as if they were breathing stale air already. Actually, it was still perfectly breathable, but the psychological result of suppressed fear couldn't be helped by mere facts.

Twenty-one hours from the time the fire had broken

out, Nora came running out of Thorndyke's office, forgetting all she had learned about traveling without gravity. Her feet flew out from under her, and she continued kicking, until Dan caught her and pulled her back to her feet. "The radio!" she gasped.

Thorndyke sailed in with a single leap, and yanked the phones to his ears. He listened, and his face fell.

"They're simply reporting on the storm. It's worse down there now, and they think it's going to last for another eighteen to twenty hours. How long can we hold out, Dr. Perez?"

"Not that long," Perez said quietly.

Thorndyke relayed the best figure at which they could guess. His shoulders were drooping as he began to taste defeat after all their efforts.

"I might as well get some sleep," Jim suggested, and there was no protest. If they had to die, it was better to sleep—if he could—than to sit here worrying about it.

Nora caught his hand, and drew him into her office. "No, Jim," she said. Her face was pinched and haggard with worry, but some of the smile managed to creep to the corners of her mouth. "Stay here with me. I can't sleep—and I need someone to talk to."

They found very little to talk about. The time ran on. They reached the thirty-hour mark, and there was still a little oxygen in the tanks, though very little. They could live for a while on the air in the hut, but that was only a small extension. The carbon-dioxide problem seemed licked, but there was nothing that could be done to replace the oxygen.

Then Thorndyke's cry brought them into his office. Only a handful were still awake. The rest were sleeping under the spell of Dr. Perez' drugs.

The engineer was bent over the radio, listening on the phones. Now he put them back and faced the few who waited.

"Mark Emmett has insisted on taking off, and he's got permission somehow. As near as I can gather, he is going to scuttle the automatic pilot and ride it up on manual controls. Does that mean anything?"

Jim nodded slowly. It meant that Emmett was a fool beyond any he'd known. It was almost impossible for a man to control a rocket, even with a waste of fuel, well enough to equal the automatics. And yet a human brain could do things no machine could equal—it could be flexible for unforeseen emergencies.

"It's the only way possible," he admitted doubtfully. "If it is possible. It won't help if his stages stick, but he might be able to ride the storm a little. It'll be a miracle if he has enough fuel to get up, though, without any left for the return."

"The next ship can bring enough as cargo for both to return," Dan said. "Well, we can't say they aren't trying."

This time there was no visible sign that they could see, though they had wasted a few precious drops of oxygen in opening the air lock and going out. The little wouldn't matter, whether Mark succeeded or not.

It was fifty minutes later when Dan pointed. At first Jim could see nothing. Then he saw it, a faint dot coming toward them. The rocket seemed to crawl up. It was turned over, waiting for the correcting blast. Now that came, obviously handled by the automatic pilot here where that could be trusted again. It was a beautiful piece of maneuvering, leaving the rocket less than five hundred feet from the station.

Perez had awakened Jerry, and the man was already in the taxi. Now it flashed across the space between them, not bothering to conserve fuel this time. There was a single figure in the open lock of the rocket, waiting for it.

Five minutes later, Jerry was back, bringing the taxi to a stop just beyond the air lock of the station. Men who looked as if they'd just been awakened were coming out and diving in. A stream of oxygen containers began pouring in through the locks, as fast as they could be worked. And behind them came Mark Emmett.

The man had lost all his dapper assurance. He staggered

as he braced himself to jump through the lock, and Jim's hand caught him and pulled him inside.

"He came alone—no copilot, no radarman," Jerry called over the phones.

"No sense," Mark muttered. "Killing one man's better than three. And I made it. I didn't think the old baby would hold. But she took it. About six ounces of fuel left, I'll bet. Mr. Thorndyke!"

Thorndyke had been standing back while Jim squeezed the hand of his friend, but now he shoved forward. Mark saw him, and gestured toward his office. "Something else to show you—in private."

Jim turned to leave at the entrance to the office, but Thorndyke shook his head. "I'm not chasing out anyone who kept this deathwatch with me. Unless you insist, Emmett?"

"Right now I wouldn't insist on living," Mark said. "I just want to get this off my chest and then find a place to curl up and sleep. Fifty-six minutes—and I feel as if I'd had to manufacture every one of them personally."

"When I believe you're here, I'll start thanking you," Thorndyke began.

Emmett shook his head. "Don't bother. My job. Here, they told me to give this to you."

From a pouch in his belt he drew out a small envelope and handed it over. Thorndyke opened it; his face drew into a doubtful frown, and then shock and anger covered it.

It was a page torn from a paper printed by the official Combine press, with a translation typed out on thin paper. The headline read:

AMERICA BUILDS SPACE STATION!

Under that was an account of how the war lords of America and the American-European Alliance were secretly building a station in space from which they hoped to drop bombs upon the peaceful citizens of the Combine. It might not have meant anything, except that it carried with it a fuzzy but recognizable picture of the station about as Jim had first seen it, and a slightly clearer copy of the diagram of its finished form, still hanging on the office wall.

"That had to come from here—nobody else could have taken the first picture," Mark said. "You've got a spy up here. And there's trouble down below."

There was obviously plenty of trouble. The Combine had furnished what proof they had to the World Congress, with an appeal to have the station declared illegal until it could be made international. They had branded it an act of war against all other nations.

It meant that there was a spy among them—and not the poor foolish man who'd spilled the sodium. He hadn't been near the station during the time when it had looked like the picture.

Mark stayed until the next ship could come up, after the storm was over, bringing his copilot and Lee Yeng. Once the strain and fatigue were over, he probably enjoyed being the hero, though he pretended he didn't. Then he went back on his own ship, as cocky as if nothing unusual had come up.

The station settled back to normal. Repairing the ruined section took up their first efforts, but it was almost worth the wasted time. The accident had forced them closer together and had turned them into a solid community with common interests. The new men who came up felt it and caught it from the others.

Now more women were coming up with the men. Nora had proved that a girl could stand space as well as any man, and there were plenty of jobs where mere physical strength was less important than the ability to do delicate, exact work for which women had always been noted. The girls fitted readily into the station life, and their presence added a feeling of social completeness that had been lacking before. Everyone seemed happier and worked harder.

Dan scowled at the fact that they had slipped behind schedule again, but he was happy at the way the work was going. On the surface, everything was as it should be. But underneath, there was a grimmer note. Jim could sense it in the thoughtful looks that were turned to him from time to time, as if someone were remembering that he had come up at about the right time to take that first picture. All of the sixty-odd men who had been there long enough were automatically suspect.

He found that the pockets in the sleeping cubicle had been searched, and he was sure that Thorndyke had some of the newer men checking on everyone.

The engineer had debated the proper procedure and had

finally shown the paper and picture to everyone. It would be easier, he thought, to catch a spy when every hand was turned against the man than to seek him out by routine methods which had already failed once on Earth. They were already fairly sure that no miniature camera was on the station now.

The big sun mirror was completed finally. The station had been set to face the Sun at all times. Eventually, it would drift away until the top no longer pointed toward the right direction, but a few careful blasts with powder rockets, such as the JATO's, would correct that.

When full power came on, it was a big event. They had been hampered badly by the inability to use any real power tools. Now the crates of machinery were broken open, and Dan supervised the setting up of a machine shop where it would be in the final station.

The station itself was a weird-looking affair now. Much of it was bare, with no metal hull around it. Here and there, the decks and power equipment were installed, and wires were being strung, along with the maze of plumbing. Water would be used to trim the final station, and to keep an even distribution of weight, since it could be pumped about easily. But it took a lot of piping to handle it.

The real job now was the beginning of the living quarters. The hut and its extensions had never been meant for more than a temporary makeshift. New quarters were being built, equipped with proper dining halls, bunks, real bathrooms, and all the luxuries of home, according to Bart. Little Terrence Rodriguez stared at the installation, and shook his head.

"Not my home," he objected. "Compared to that, this will be a palace."

It would hardly be palatial. It was modeled on the living accommodations of the atomic submarines, which meant that everything took up the minimum space. But it would enable men to live in reasonable comfort, once it was completed and the station was set to spinning.

That was another project they were trying to hasten. In actual operation, the station had been intended to revolve around its hub once each twenty-two seconds. This would create a centrifugal force, weak near the center, but growing stronger until at the outer edge it was nearly a third of the normal pressure of Earth's gravitation. It would make it possible for the men who were to work there to live normal lives. Without that, the new installations were useless.

Jim was busy helping to install the inner layer—the fabric sheathing that would keep in the air. Around that, and held away by studs placed at definite intervals, would be the outer metal hull. It was expected that the thin plates would halt nearly all the tiny meteorites which might strike the station, while also reflecting back the Sun's radiation, except for certain patches where they could expose darkened sections when they wanted to, to regulate temperature.

The amount of equipment was almost indescribable. It lay scattered about, some of it waiting for further completion of the station, other parts waiting for the men who would be skilled enough to install it. There was radar gear, television gear, and all the complexities of electronics. The station would have to be able to communicate with the ground at all times, and to spot anything in space. There was even a mirror for an astronomical telescope. This would be mounted in a separate little substation, like a doghouse in the back, where it could be set to hold a more rigidly fixed position than was possible on the station itself. It would also be used to study the ground below, with television cameras to relay what was seen to the main station.

Also, there were all the installations for military purposes. Jim avoided thinking about them. He knew that it was necessary to have them. Without such power, war was inevitable eventually on Earth; but so long as the United States had the power of releasing atomic and hydrogen bombs from the station on any nation which started an attack, there would be no attack. It was the one case where military power could bring peace.

The framework for the spokes and the central hub had

already been connected, and two specialists had finally been found who could handle the elevators that would connect the hub and the outer wheel, without going space crazy.

The more they accomplished, the more apparently remained to be done. With the use of power tools to cut and handle the parts needed, the work took on greater speed. But again, space presented its own problems. A grinder seemed like a simple device. Yet when it was turned on in the machine shop and Jim went to sharpen a pair of special scissors with which he trimmed the fabric lining, it proved a near disaster. The bits of metal and abrasive flew out in a straight line—and then drifted and ricocheted around. Without gravity, there was nothing to bring them to rest, and they made moving about in a flimsy space suit nearly impossible. The use of the lathe or heavier tools was clearly unthinkable.

Thorndyke listened as Dan presented the reasons for spinning the station ahead of time, and shook his head.

"It'll wobble, Dan. If it isn't exactly balanced, it will wobble like a top running down, and like an off-center wheel. Remember, it won't spin around the hub—it'll spin around the center of mass. If one side is light and the other heavy, it will have a center somewhere between the hub and the heavy side. And we don't have the trim tanks ready."

"So what?" Dan asked. "So it wouldn't work for the men who want to do scientific experiments. And so our weight will fluctuate a little. That doesn't matter now. We've placed most of the heavy stuff in pretty fair balance already. If we don't get some weight, though, we'll probably never be able to keep some of the technicians we're going to need."

Thorndyke considered. "You've got a point, Dan. I've been trying to get some men here who've been working on plant culture to replenish the air. But they can't find anyone who could stand raw space. And I guess it would be pretty hard to set up a bunch of plants in water if the water wasn't held down by some substitute for gravity. Let me think it over."

He had plenty to think about. There was the matter of the spy, the complaint before the World Congress, which still hadn't come up yet, the delay in reaching the schedule the contract called for—and the eternal difficulty of finding men who could do the needed work under the conditions.

The next day Thorndyke called Dan over, and nodded. "Spin it!"

They had a supply of larger rocket tubes than those used by hand with which they hoped to set it spinning. These were to be placed along the outer edge of the wheel, like the little rockets on a pin wheel. When they were set off, the pin-wheel effect would be complete, and the station should begin turning as smoothly as a phonograph record on the turntable.

Jim had wanted to be in on the job, and Dan nodded when he applied. He sighed. "I've been trying to get you a job as foreman of one of the gangs, boy. But I can't even put you up for lead man. Now that we're out of the worst part, they keep crying for specialists. Bart and I'd be down-graded if they didn't have contracts on us, I expect. But Thorndyke likes you. If there's any job you want, you'll get it."

"And you'd better tell this Jim he's a darned fool, Dan," Bart said. "Setting those rockets off isn't going to be a picnic."

Jim soon found that Bart was right. Each of the rockets had to be tested carefully against a compression scale to make sure it was adjusted to exactly the same thrust; otherwise, the stronger ones would have put uneven pressure on the edge of the wheel with some danger of buckling sections of it.

The rockets had to be lined up precisely. Dan and Bart insisted on working on the job. They had brought Jerry Wales, the station taxi jockey. One more was needed, and Jim suggested Terrence Rodriguez; the little man could be depended on to follow orders, and he had enough sense to question orders that sounded wrong before following them.

Also, he could outwork most other men without complaining.

"You sure of that, kid?" Bart asked. "Not that I'm questioning Terrence. He's a good guy. But how would you know about the others?"

Jim thought it over slowly. He had to admit that there was entirely too much truth in the implied answer to the question. He'd been far too busy to pay much attention to what the other men were doing, particularly since the number had been swelling beyond the original group.

"You might have made lead man," Bart went on. "Dan didn't tell you the whole truth. He suggested it to Thorndyke, who asked me. I turned you down, kid. Nope. I'm not apologizing. I'm just suggesting that when you get to know more about people and to work with them, nothing will keep you from being lead man. Until then, the responsibility of having to learn to watch them would drive you crazy. Sure, I think Terrence is a good man. But next time, I'd like to have you suggest a dozen."

Jim swallowed it, nodding glumly. He'd told himself the same often enough. But knowing about a fault and correcting it weren't the same. "I'll try, Bart," he promised. "And—and thanks!"

But he wasn't sure he wanted to be lead man for a group. He'd had enough trouble with the sodium painting when there were two under him. As long as he was doing the job himself, he could be sure it was done as nearly right as he knew how; with others doing it, he could never be sure.

He turned it over in his mind, resolving to watch the other men around him. Then they began installing the rockets, and there was too much to do for thought.

He went around the whole edge when it was done, checking. Dan trusted him for that, as well as the foreman trusted himself, and it felt good. Jim was nearly around the circle, coasting with short, sure jets from the rocket tube to keep him circling, when he spotted trouble.

Three of the tubes were on wrong. Even to his eye, they were out of line. He called Bart, who came at once.

"On Terrence's work," he said. "Wait—wait, don't fly off the handle, kid. I inspected them myself after Terrence did them. They were right. Anyone could have come by here and twisted them. We've got five hundred men up here now, and it could have been nearly any single soul you could think of, except maybe a few of the technicians who can't use rocket tubes. Well, we'll fly patrol from now on. Let's fix them."

They aligned them again, making sure they were fastened securely. With the blasts tilted, they could have heaved one section of the wheel upward, upsetting the whole spin and even twisting the frame. It could have meant weeks of repair work.

Dan vetoed the guard duty. "Clear out the men from the hull," he ordered after a brief conference with Thorndyke. "All of them. Put the greenhorns between men who are able to take space, and get them out of the way. We'll spin it now!"

It took an hour to get everyone cleared out, and some of the newer men were having a hard time of it. But there was no time to worry about that. The wire that connected all the rocket tubes to the main switch was in place. Dan, Bart, Terrence, Jerry and Jim fastened themselves to the framework of the hub, and Dan reached for the switch.

It wasn't as smooth as it should have been, but there was an instant response as the tubes began blasting. Slowly, the great wheel began to turn, picking up rotational speed. It was unbalanced, as Thorndyke had said, and it wobbled, but the motion was bearable at the hub.

Then Thorndyke's voice reached them over the phones. "Two rockets on section twenty-seven aren't firing, Dan! And it looks as if the frame is going to buckle from the pressure of the others. Better cut jets."

"Cut jets . . ." Dan growled at the idea. Once they cut the jets, there was no way to get them started again. They didn't have multiple starters, like the hand tubes. It would mean doing the whole job over.

Bart stood up, staring at the section where the tubes

had mysteriously failed. "Maybe we could get replacements . . ." he began.

Jim swung around, and braced himself for a take-off toward the tube dump. But Terrence was ahead of him, dipping down with quick blasts from his rocket tube. He caught up a couple of the bigger tubes, and headed back —but toward the outer edge of the wheel.

Dan's voice cut off Jim's protest. "Get back here, Terrence. With this spinning, you'd be cut in two from the blasts before you could correct your speed and land outside!"

The little man swung back reluctantly. Jim reached for the tubes, but Bart plucked them out of his hands. "It's my idea, kid," he said. "I'm going."

He used his hand tube to sail across to the inner side of the wheel. It was wobbling, and matching speed was almost impossible. Bart came as close as he could, then caught a beam. Jim felt his arms ache in sympathy, but the big man made it. He crawled through the open section of girders, heading for the defective tubes.

It was delicate work, lining up the new tubes. But a minute later his voice came over the phones. "Blast!"

Dan threw the switch, and they could see the faint edge of the trail from the new tubes. Bart stood up cautiously, turning. He was swaying, unused to any kind of gravity for the last few months. He reached for a beam.

The section of the wheel where he was had reached its outer limit of wobble, and now began moving in, like the edge of a phonograph record, with an off-center hole moving the narrow part into view. Bart grabbed for the beam, and his body swayed outward. He jerked his foot to secure a firmer bracing, and missed.

Jim felt a scream tear from his throat, but there was nothing he could do. Bart's other foot tore loose, and the man shot out from the wheel. The rocket tubes spun by him, blasting like a giant pin wheel, sending up flames from the fabric of his suit.

His voice cut into their earphones, surprised, shocked

and almost instantly level again. "I—I . . . Jim, kid—what I said about people . . ."

It died out as the air went out of his suit. When they reached him, Bart Smith was dead.

They buried Bart in space. It had been his own idea, Dan told them, and it was going to be done the way Bart wanted. Nobody objected. They put the body in a new space suit, onto which Jim had attached a framework to hold six of the bigger rocket tubes, and aimed him toward the outer planets. In his life, he'd gone as far as any man could; in death, he'd be the first one to reach the orbit of Mars. Thorndyke had figured it out, and assured them that the six tubes would give him enough acceleration from the station for that.

It was Terrence who recited the ceremony over him, drawing the sad, traditional words out of his memory. There should have been a chaplain, and would be soon, but they couldn't wait. And at last the little man looked up from the final prayer and nodded, while Jim set off the tubes. For a time they could see the diminishing trails of the rockets, and then there was only empty space.

"God will know where he is," Terrence said finally, and Jim nodded his head.

But the work went on, even though Jim felt the sorrow more deeply than most. Dan said nothing, but gave up his own single quarters to move in with the boy for the few brief days before they could finish the more luxurious quarters and move into them.

The station was spinning. It wobbled and danced around a spot not at its hub, but there was a feeling of weight again near the outside of the wheel. Liquids flowed down, and food remained on open dishes. The weight of the men fluctuated, but it was slow enough a change not to bother them.

They were concentrating on finishing the outer hull now. Jim pitched in with a greater effort. For a time, he tried to hold a part of his mind to the last job Bart had left him, but it kept slipping off to the work. It was easier to forget when he was busy, and he wanted to forget.

Nora watched him, worrying over him. With the presence of gravity, the boxes of games had been broken open to provide some entertainment for the men. She found a game which involved putting letters onto little squares to form words, and challenged him to a running contest. When that didn't work, she tried another. Finally, she gave up, and put him to reading to her out of some of the books Thorndyke had, making him explain what she couldn't understand.

And she talked about the people in the station. She seemed to know all of them, though most of them were just names to him.

"Jerry Wales is getting to be a problem," she told him one time after his work shift. "I suppose I shouldn't tell you, but maybe you can do something. He keeps taking sedatives. He says he can't sleep without them. Ever since Bart died, he's been like that. Of course, he used to take them at the beginning of the station, but I thought he'd gotten over that."

Jim muttered something, and started to forget it. Then he hesitated. "Right after Bart's death?"

She nodded. "He came the day before, but just for a normal dose. Afterward, he wanted a double dose. And he's still taking it. I'm going to report him to Dr. Perez if this goes on."

"Let him have it!" Jim suggested suddenly. "Let him have all he wants, Nora, but be sure to keep a record of it!"

He had nothing but a vague suspicion to go on, and he knew he was being unfair. But the hunt was still on for the spy, and no one had turned up anything. There had been those rocket tubes, bent out of line. And the failure of the two that had led to Bart's death was something he had never understood, unless someone had drained away part of the fuel.

Jerry had had ample opportunities. He'd been part of their group. So had Terrence, for that matter—but Terrence hadn't been on the station during the time when the picture could have been taken, while Jerry had. He groped around in his memory, looking for other things. Something seemed to be missing.

Finally he nodded faintly. He'd seen Jerry talking to the man who'd let the sodium spill into the lock. It proved nothing—Jerry talked to a lot of people. But a few words about what a fuss-budget Jim was, dropped at the right time, might have overcome all the warning Jim had tried to give the man. It had always seemed strange that some of that warning hadn't penetrated.

Besides, who would have had a better chance to take a picture of the whole station? Jerry had jockeyed the taxi since it had been sent up, and the picture must have been taken from some distance. A miniature camera might have been hidden inside some bale sent up, marked so he could locate it. It would have been easy for him to slip it into the air lock of the rocket on another trip. If the camera was small enough, nobody would have noticed it; some of them were no bigger than the joint of a finger.

Jim had nothing but circumstantial evidence, he knew, and he was fixing the worst possible charge on a man because of that. But he couldn't get it out of his mind. If Jerry was guilty, there would be more trouble. It might result in death for hundreds of people. If the boy was innocent, he might be able to establish some proof; at least he wouldn't be condemned without more proof than Jim had.

Yet he liked Jerry. The man was a genius with the taxi, and he had a quick, nervous sense of humor that had brightened a lot of dull evenings. He'd put on mock-aerial shows, when there was no gravity, for all of them. And he'd even taken Jim along in the taxi several times and let him try his hand at it.

Jim sweated it out, telling no one. He'd been brought up with the belief that a "rat" was the lowest form of life— that no man ever ratted on another, and that even thieves had their honor. He knew it wasn't entirely true, but the emotional reaction to carrying tales still stuck. Twice he made up his mind to see Thorndyke, and both times he couldn't do it. The ethics of the situation were far too tangled in his head.

It was Nora who finally settled the problem. She was frowning when Jim went into her office. "It's Jerry," she said. "I let him have the sedatives, like you said. But I already gave him one double dose, and then he came back for another. He's going to pieces, Jim."

Jim quieted her, making up a false job that Jerry had to do to calm her suspicions. But when he left, he headed for Thorndyke's room. If there was any connection between the sedatives and Jerry's work as a spy, it must mean something was about to happen.

The engineer was still up. "Come in, Jim," he said quickly. "It's the last night before we move to our new quarters, and somehow I can't sleep on the floor very comfortably. It was all right when there was no gravity—but even at one-third weight, that's too hard now. Want a game of chess?"

It was an honor the man sometimes offered to Dan, and ordinarily Jim would have jumped at it. He was fairly good at chess, and it had been years since he'd played much of it—since his father had died, in fact. But he shook his head.

It took him half an hour of hedging and false starts before he could overcome his scruples. But it finally came out in a rush. Thorndyke listened without expression until he had finished.

"Ethics are hard to explain, Jim," he said. "I had a course in them at college once. I didn't think I learned anything at the time. Now, I'm not so sure. You can't betray a friend who isn't your friend! And in times like these, you sometimes have to make sure that the good things will survive by sailing pretty close to the wind. Nobody likes the security checks we go through—but they're necessary, even when they hurt some people and can't keep out all the spies.

"And don't forget that the other guy isn't evil, in his own eyes. You can like an enemy. He may even be a nice guy, with as many ethics as you have. Maybe Jerry—if he's guilty—honestly believes that this station will ruin the whole future of his people or the world. Maybe he's willing to kill himself for what he thinks is right. You and I think he's wrong, of course. And sometimes, because we think so, we have to do things we don't want to."

He stood up, pacing about the little room, and the sight of a man walking was still strange enough to Jim now for him to follow the engineer's steps with his eyes. "Jim, if you're right, he's about to try something pretty big. Well, he's going out to pick up some high-priority material from a rocket tomorrow—stuff that has something to do with the handling and aiming of the bombs when they're sent up here. I can't tell you any more. I probably should turn him in—or lock him up at once. But it's important to find out what he intends. How'd you like to ride along in the taxi with him?"

"I wouldn't like it," Jim said. "But I'll go if you want. Only I'll probably make a lousy spy."

"Don't try to be one. Just do your job and keep your eyes open. If you find anything suspicious, hit him first! Now . . . how about that game of chess? There's time, before you need to turn in."

Thorndyke beat him badly, but it was good medicine for his nerves. Jim slept better than usual, in spite of the coming mission. In the morning, he managed to seem surprised when Dan called him over and ordered him to help Jerry. If there was any reaction on the taxi jockey's part, Jim couldn't see it.

The rocket came up about noon, as they kept time on the station—which meant the same time as that used on Johnston Island. Jim was surprised to see that Gantry was listed as its pilot. Apparently the man had been able to bail out of his exploding rocket and had been rescued in time. It was news that had probably gone all over the station, but he had been too preoccupied to notice it.

The rocket pilots .had become clever about their approaches to the station now, and were able to shade the correcting blast of the automatic pilot almost by instinct, so that they seldom needed to jockey closer to the station after they matched course. This was a particularly smooth job, but it brought the ship a good mile from the station.

Jerry shrugged. "Must mean something special on board," he guessed. "They sometimes get coy when they don't want any of the regular men coming over to exchange gossip. Want to take the taxi out for practice this time, Jim?"

Jim's fingers itched for the controls. It was the closest to the actual piloting of a space ship that he could hope for. But he turned it down within himself, knowing he'd be in a better position to watch if he took the seat behind and stayed in the rear.

"I've got a touch of a headache," he said. Then, because it never did any harm to mix as much truth into a story as possible, on the chance that the listener might know something about it, he tried to act as if he were boasting. "I was up playing chess with Thorndyke. I guess I tried too hard."

"Oh! Who won?" Jerry didn't seem very interested. He was frowning, and his thin face was set into a tautness that left his lips nearly white.

"He did. I'm out of practice." He let it go at that, and Jerry only nodded. They were nearly at the ship. He suddenly stood up, indicating that Jim should take the controls, and went forward toward the lock.

Most of the piloting of the little ferry had been finished. Jim let it drift in, correcting the slow motion of the nose to the side with the gyroscope. It was a perfect contact, with a little momentum that was soaked up easily enough. Jerry jerked open the seals and sprang forward.

Jim frowned as he lost sight of the jockey. Then he caught a glimpse of the man in the polished inner door of the air lock. It wasn't as clear as it might have been, but he could make out enough. Jerry stood talking idly with Gantry for a few seconds, and then nodded.

"Okay, if it's so special, I'll give you a hand with it. Go ahead, I'll catch up. I want to make sure everything's clear here." Jerry turned back, appearing to study the interior of the taxi. There was a wrench on the floor, and he moved it aside. Then he turned and headed back toward the rocket.

Jim barely caught the flicker of white in time to see that it was a slim piece of paper in Jerry's hand. In the door of the lock, his image hesitated for a split second, while the hand with the paper shot out toward the big silicone-rubber gasket.

It was the perfect hiding place! Soft and resilient, it would give enough for anything thin to slip under it, and nobody would think to search there. Yet any man who went near the ship to service it could remove the paper without being seen, simply by resting his hand on the gasket as he went through the lock.

Jim's throat tightened. But it wasn't enough. There must be more than that—or he'd have no evidence that he couldn't have planted himself. He waited, while the seconds ticked by. Then he saw Jerry coming out with a large box balanced delicately in his hands. Behind the jockey, Gantry's laugh sounded.

"Oh, come on, Jerry. It may be special, but it won't explode. You might as well toss it down and give me a hand with a few other crates."

Jerry shook his head firmly, while his lips were even whiter, and he lowered the box as if it were filled with dynamite. He seemed to forget that it had already taken the smashing pressure of several gravities of acceleration. Nothing shipped by rocket could be too subject to trouble from a little shock. "Nope, can't. Thorndyke told me to pick this up and bring it to him without delay."

He began closing the lock, and Gantry shrugged easily. It was obviously none of his business. He'd brought it, and that took care of his work.

"Cast off," Jerry said carefully.

Jim began swinging the ship about for the blast away from the rocket. "Where to? Thorndyke's new quarters?"

"No, that was just to cover for Gantry. This is special stuff. It's a control for the trim tanks, to stop the station wobbling—or I guess it is. Thorndyke told me to store it in the bomb-bay section."

It was partly true, Jim knew, and none of it was completely a lie. It was supposed to be stored there, and Jerry's guess as to its use wasn't too fantastic, if he didn't know. But it would be easy to move it from there to the turbine room—where a bomb might break pipes that would send gaseous mercury through most of the enclosed part of the ship—enough to kill everyone.

"Better take the controls," Jim suggested. "My head's getting worse. I'll take care of the box for you, if it's so delicate."

"Who said it was delicate?" Jerry snapped tightly. "It's just a hunk of machinery. And nobody needs to watch it."

Jim slipped back to the rear seat, his eyes going to the box. He felt the blast from the taxi rocket, and his eyes jerked back. It was one thing to know that any explosive was safe enough to handle if it had passed the test of rocket shipment; it was another matter to ride with what might be a live bomb.

He jerked his eyes back—and looked squarely into a tiny, deadly pistol in Jerry's hands.

"Yeah," Jerry said slowly. "Yeah, Jim. You're right. It's a bomb. But *you* won't have to keep worrying."

Chapter 12 *Earthside*

Jerry's finger squeezed down on the trigger. Jim threw himself sideways in a desperate lunge, just as there was a deafening explosion. The bullet spanged against the rocket motor, ricocheted off to strike the air lock, rebounded, and spent itself in the seat of the pilot's chair. Jim bounced back from a wall, and braced himself for another shot.

But Jerry had forgotten that guns have a recoil equal to the force of the bullet. Shock ran over the man's face as he went spinning back to crash against the air lock, with the gun sailing from his fingers. He rebounded.

Jim grabbed the back of a seat and heaved himself forward. He caught the jockey just as the man was groping for a handhold. In weightless fighting, Jerry would have the advantage normally. But Jim gave him no chance. One of his hands went around the other's neck, and his other fist lashed forward, back and forward again. He kept striking, never giving the other a chance to regain his balance.

Jerry buckled, his body growing limp.

Jim ripped the straps from the second seat and lashed the unconscious man firmly against the back of the seat where he could do nothing if he revived. His own face was bleeding from scratches he hadn't known he'd received, and he could feel the blood pounding against his temples, while the big artery in his throat throbbed rapidly.

He buckled himself into the pilot seat and located the station. The taxi had drifted nearer to it than to the rocket ship. Jim cranked the gyroscope, and began the tricky job of trying to match speed with the outside of the spinning station. He'd forgotten that the spin would be erratic until he drew up to it and began trying to come alongside one of the ports. He made two passes at it, with poor success.

The third time, a man leaped for the taxi with a rope.

A minute later, Jim felt the little ship being drawn back toward the port, and he relaxed while they anchored it. He lifted the semiconscious Jerry out of the straps and began dragging him through the locks.

Thorndyke was waiting inside, and Jim reported hastily, while other men took control of Jerry. Nora came up, bawling out both the head engineer and Jim for trying to play counterspy, but her hands were gentle as she began treating the scratches on his head.

He shook her off and went out with Dan and two others to move the box out into space and check on its contents. But there was no surprise when they found that it held enough high explosive to wreck half the station, together with a timing device. The gun alone had been evidence enough.

Jim got back to find Gantry arguing with Thorndyke. The rocket pilot was finishing a flat denial of something, and the engineer shrugged and turned to Jim. "Gantry won't carry prisoners—says he isn't equipped to play guard. You'll have to go Earthside, Jim, unless you have strong objections."

Jim shrugged. "No objections, I guess, sir," he said. He had no relish for the job, but someone had to do it. And since he'd gotten mixed up in it already, it might as well be he. It was an ugly business, totally lacking in the romance that was supposed to surround spy affairs.

Jerry was brought out to the taxi by two of the men, his wrists tied firmly. He sneered at Thorndyke but went quietly back with Jim and Gantry while the engineer piloted the taxi clumsily out to the rocket. There they strapped the prisoner down to one of the contour chairs and Jim took the one alongside.

Gantry checked his position carefully, and then the rockets went on for fifteen seconds, cutting their speed to fourteen thousand, slowing them enough for Earth to begin pulling them down. The station began to move away ahead of them as they drifted downward. They would now have fifty minutes of descent in which nothing could be done.

Gantry stared back at Jerry. "He doesn't look like a lousy Combine man," he said. "I used to think he was a good kid."

"Who says I'm a Combine man?" Jerry asked sharply. He scowled at them. "I'm as good an American as the rest of you—better, maybe."

"Sure, Jerry," Jim agreed heavily. "At least more generous with pictures of the station. The Combine must have liked that."

Jerry stared at them, hot anger on his face. Then he shrugged, and his face returned to its normal scowl. "Okay, I'm cooked anyway. Do you really want to know why I did it, or don't you?"

He accepted their nods, and his eyes went blank as he leaned back to stare at the tiny image of the station on one of the screens.

"Okay. I had a friend—you know about him already, so that's not spilling anything. And I suppose there's no way I can keep him from tipping himself off, now. He used to be with the circus, too, before my family's accident. That was on the level, by the way. We traveled over most of the world. And every place we went, we saw people going without food so their countries could buy more nice bombs for the soldier boys to play with. We used to talk about it, and about that big, bright, beautiful dream everybody had —an island up in the sky where they could stock up more nice bombs. Only from that, they could kill almost everybody. We made up our minds that if we had any chance, we'd blow it to bits before they blew up the world. We were just kids, see? We thought it was something we'd never have a crack at.

"So what do they do but draft my friend? And he gets sent to Johnston Island to be a messenger for the brass. When he saw what was going on, he got in touch with me— never mind how. And we decided we meant what we'd said. He worked himself in solid on the field. I took me a good course in rockets—I was at Central Tech when you came there, but you probably wouldn't remember me. And I made sure I was good at it, but not quite good enough

102

to be a pilot. So—well, when they hinted there might be a job, I played it the way they wanted, and they sent me up. It wasn't hard to get the job on the taxi—all like stealing candy from kids. And if I hadn't had a string of bad luck, the station would be blooey by now. That picture was turned over just to give somebody else a chance to knock out the station, but the Combine didn't do what we expected, when we proved what was going on. And that's all."

Jim stared at him incredulously. "Why?"

"Why?" Jerry grimaced and shook his head. "You can't see it at all, can you? I told you, though. Because all your pretty station is ever going to be is a launching platform for bombs. A place to plot out the murder of women and kids. A million more guys will go hungry when they could live in palaces for what it costs. And then the bombs will fall."

"We wouldn't use the bombs unless we had to," Jim pointed out. But he knew it was useless. No argument could ever convince a fanatic. "And there are a lot of other uses for a station."

"Sure. Sure there are. But the real use is murder. Do you think they're going to get all that power up there and never use it? When did they ever not use it? Didn't they use the atom bomb? Let anyone disagree with the country that has the station, and watch the pressure go on. Maybe it all starts with fine ideals—we got the station, and now there'd better be peace. Twenty years later, it changes to another tune—we got the station, so don't argue with us. And fifty years later, the whole world better play slave. Only it won't play slave, so it gets blown up! How blind can you be?"

"Let him rave, Jim," Gantry said. "It's the same line that wants to stop all progress because all new scientific developments can be used for war. When a man's afraid, it's easy to call the rest of the world names."

It was more than that, Jim knew. There was just enough truth in it to give a fanatic an absolute conviction that he was right. There was a danger to having all that power up there—but there was more danger in letting things go as they were or allowing the station to wait until some madman gained power to build it.

There was never any answer to a man who felt he had a mission to go around killing others to save the world.

They touched the upper atmosphere then, and went on gliding down to a height of fifty miles, with their speed now over eighteen thousand miles an hour. Gantry turned to his controls and began sweating it out. He had to hold them in a long, flat glide where the friction of the air could slowly reduce their speed to a safe level. If he dropped too rapidly, the thicker air would have resistance enough to burn them to a cinder, like a meteor. If he held them in the very thin air too long, their speed would carry them out again, and it would all have to be done over. Here he could count on no help from the automatic pilot.

They went downward slowly, in a course calculated to take them more than halfway around the world. Some of the screens had a reddish glow now, and Jim knew that it was from their own hull. During the rush down through the air, they would reach a temperature of thirteen hundred degrees Fahrenheit, and would glow a bright cherry-red.

But the hull had been designed to stand that. The inside of the ship grew warmer, but the insulation held. Then a sigh from Gantry told him that the worst was over. Now they had slowed to a normal air speed, and were in denser air. The atmosphere here would soon soak up the heat of the hull at any normal cruising speed. It was a long, difficult maneuver, but it saved fuel. If they'd had to take enough fuel to land by rocket, the whole trip would have been impossible; this way, it was fairly practical.

The ship cut through clouds, and one of the screens showed Johnston Island ahead. They continued to slow, until they were landing on the water at a lower speed than many of the regular liners.

A small tug ran out to haul them in to the dock, where the rocket would be lifted out, put back into top condition, and raised onto another first and second stage.

A familiar figure was waiting on the dock when Jim stepped out with the prisoner. Jim stuck out his hand, and

John Mattern grabbed it. The tall, rough-featured man studied the boy from top to bottom, and grinned.

"You look good, Stanley. I guess it agrees with you."

"I feel good," Jim agreed. "You should come up some time."

Mattern shook his head. "Not me! This the man I'm supposed to pick up?"

Jim turned Jerry over to him, and accepted an envelope which a waiting messenger was holding out to him. He saw that it was a voucher for a room and food, a list of things he could and could not do, and an order to report to the medical examiner's office. He considered that for a while, and then shrugged. He'd been examined enough.

At the small bank, they were cordial enough, and caused no trouble. He drew out a hundred dollars, and headed down the street that served as a shopping district for the men who were posted on the Island. But his first step was at a restaurant where he could order all the things he'd missed.

He sat down, puffing. His legs ached already, and he felt as if he'd done a hard day's work in walking the few blocks. Earth was heavy! The food was better than they had at the station, but the first few bites sated his craving; he hadn't been really hungry.

He bought a few light trinkets, trusting in his friendship with the pilots to let him get by with them. There was a new mechanical pencil for Dan, a box of expensive powder for Nora, and a watch for Terrence. For himself, he could think of very little. He'd never been tied down with many material possessions, and hadn't missed them on the station.

He found the little hotel, and presented his papers. The clerk sent him to a room on the second floor. He found the steps a torture. He supposed a man could get used to living on Earth again, but he was wondering whether it was worth it. And the bed was supposed to be soft, but it felt like solid concrete to him. His back began to ache, and one of his legs fell asleep from the pressure of the other.

Somehow, though, he slept through the night, to get up

in the morning hardly more refreshed than when he'd lain down.

Again, the food was the one virtue he could find. It was far better than they could have on the station, where everything had to be taken up in condensed form. The taste of real milk was something of a revelation to him. He checked his watch, found he had time to kill, and wandered into a record store. He bought several records, knowing that he could never take them with him, but because it seemed wrong somehow to waste the store's facilities listening to them without buying anything. That was another thing he'd missed at the station, where they had no music.

When he came out, there were headlines staring him right in the face that jerked his thoughts back to reality.

U. S. ANNOUNCES IT HAS SPACE STATION!

There was a big picture of what the completed station would look like spread over four columns. It was a somewhat idealized view, with a cutaway section that had been filled in by some artist who seemed to think scientific instruments had to be fifteen feet tall, and full of oscilloscope traces and lightning bolts. But it was correct enough generally, showing the big globe and the outer ring, or wheel.

There was little news to the story. It simply gave the bare fact that the United States had a space station under construction in a two-hour orbit, confirming the news the Combine had released. The writer had puffed it up with everything he could find from the books, but no reason for the announcement was given, nor were any significant facts.

Jim whistled. The leak to the Combine through Jerry's friend must have hurt plenty, to make them break the story officially; either that, or the foreign situation was getting too tense, and they were using the news of the station to give themselves a cooling-off period while the other powers thought it over.

Jim threw the paper away, after making sure that there was no other information. He bought one of the little four-page local papers, but it had the same announcement, except that it was colored to readers already aware of the station. On the fourth page, there was a little story of a man shot while looting one of the rockets. He was listed as a fuel truck driver, and had been caught inside the last rocket to land; when he tried to escape, the guard had shot him.

So Jerry's friend had not only tried to collect the piece of paper, but hadn't had enough sense to surrender when caught!

He was stopped at the field. He showed his badge, and the guard examined it, then shook his head. "Where's your medical clearance?"

"I've already been cleared," Jim told him. "I'm going back! Ask Mark Emmett, or Gantry. Any of the pilots know me."

The guard nodded. "Sure, I know you, too. I've been expecting you. But you were supposed to report to medical for an examination. I can't let you in here without a certificate."

Jim tried arguing, but it didn't work. Finally he shrugged and gave up. "Okay, if I have to I suppose I have to. Any chance of thumbing a ride with one of the jeeps?"

"Sure. Tansley!" The guard waved his arm, and one of the jeeps cruised over. "Sam, take the boy down to medical!"

He'd missed the rocket back, Jim realized. He should have followed orders in the first place. But he didn't like all this insistence on a medical inspection. He was remembering the fact that he'd nearly failed the first one; and he had a pretty fair idea that this wouldn't be a casual, routine inspection.

Chapter 13   *Errand Boy*

It was a thorough examination. Three doctors worked Jim over from top to bottom, now and then exchanging comments that he couldn't understand. He was forced to bend over, open his mouth, stare at figures on a card, and do ten knee bends on one leg. The last almost threw him, and he could hear his heart pounding wildly afterward. He wondered why the doctor bothered to use the stethoscope.

"Tachycardia," the oldest one said calmly. "Jim, you're the first man we've had a chance to test after any prolonged continuous stay up there. There are a lot of things we need to know about the effects of space, and you're giving us some of the answers. Hmmm. Cough. Now, again!"

It wasn't encouraging. They needed a guinea pig, and they'd been reluctant to pass him the first time. Finally one of them nodded, though, indicating the examination was over. Jim moved toward his clothes. One of the doctors went into an inner office. The second doctor followed, leaving the oldest one alone with Jim.

The man studied his notes for a minute more, and then looked up with a smile. "You're not in good shape in a lot of ways, Jim. You weren't in the first place, when we passed you against our better judgment. But . . . well, there doesn't seem to be anything new wrong with you that couldn't be fixed by a few weeks of exercise down here. I guess if you made out the first time, you'll do it again." He signed something with a flourish. "Here's your certificate."

Jim heaved a long sigh of relief and began climbing into his clothes, while the doctor went into his private office and came out in a simple business suit. "They've been holding up the rocket for you, and we can't keep them waiting forever. Come on with me, and I'll drive you over to the field."

He talked casually as he drove. It was obvious that he'd been one of the men who'd dreamed of space travel back in the days when even the V-2 was impossible. Now he'd mellowed and was enjoying the idea that others were doing what he had never had a chance to accomplish. And under it all was another strain of thought, a bitterness that was somehow an acceptance of the trouble that was brewing on Earth.

"It comes and it goes," he said. "Sometimes it gets worse than others. But I've found that when the human animal gets himself into the deepest pit, he's apt to come charging up out of it the fastest. Well, here we are."

Jim got out and held a hand toward the old doctor. "Thank you, sir," he said, knowing that he meant his thanks for the second chance to go up above the atmosphere. The man chuckled, accepting it, and drove off.

Mark Emmett was waiting again, as he had been waiting so long ago when Jim had first gone up. Now, though, it seemed like an old routine. The moving ladder rolled forward, lifting them up. It had been improved since the last time; it made the lift the whole way, with no need for rope ladders.

Inside the rocket, there were two other passengers, new men who stared at Jim as if trying to see what made him tick. But his thoughts were all on getting back. He answered their questions as best he could until Mark signaled take-off. Then he snapped back against the contour seat and tried to relax.

The acceleration could never be pleasant, but it was a smooth trip, and Mark had gained experience in the months that had passed. He no longer trusted wholly to the automatic pilot; now he fiddled with it as they rose, feeding in new figures that slightly modified its course. His muscles seemed to have hardened tremendously, and the acceleration no longer hampered his movements.

Fifty-six minutes from the take-off, they were matching the orbit and speed of the space station, and only a few hundred feet away. Jim stood up with Mark, and they began putting on their suits. "Better get into your space suits," Jim said casually to the new men. "The taxi isn't too reliable now, from what I saw last. Grab our shoulders in the air lock and we'll swim you over!"

Mark chuckled, but nodded. Jim waited until one of the men had a good grip, put his own hands behind the man's knees, and jumped. It was only four hundred feet, and for that distance he had no need of the usual rocket tube. He had aimed himself to arrive at the hub, where there was no spin. He caught one of the cords, pulled himself up, and nodded. While he'd been gone, they had finished the covering on one of the spokes and the big globe of the hub. There was only one air lock now, at the hub.

Jim guided the new man down the big tube of the spoke, making sure he used the handholds. Gravity seemed to increase with each step from the weightlessness at the center to the maximum weight at the outer edge of the doughnut. Once they reached the living quarters, he turned the man over to another whose job was breaking in newcomers and headed toward his own bunk.

Then he cleared his lungs and sniffed. Home! The air was stale, with the smell of oil from the generators mixed with the odor of human bodies. But it seemed good to Jim.

Dan came in as he was putting away his few purchases. "Hi, boy! I heard you were back. What do they think of the news down there?"

"Who knows?" Jim answered him. "All I got was what the medics thought of me. It seems I'm a hopeless invalid, but good enough for space."

Dan chuckled. Then he saw the pencil Jim was holding, and dropped onto the bunk, shaking his head as if it had been a deed to a gold mine. "You shouldn't have done it," he kept repeating, but his face was beaming.

Nora was ecstatic with her gift, and Terrence refused to believe the watch was for him. Jim wished he'd thought to get something for some of the others. The absence of luxuries here had made everything triply valuable, and the rocket could have handled the few extra pounds.

There was a message for him to see Thorndyke, and he went down to the engineer's office. The man was frowning down at the messages from the rocket, but he looked up and held out a hand to Jim.

"How'd you like to take over the taxi?" he asked. "You've had a little experience, which is more than the rest of us can say. No, wait a minute." He pulled one of the papers over to him and studied it, worry and disgust on his face. "It's going to be a different job, Jim. The government is picking up its option on the military parts of the station at once. They haven't bothered to extend our deadline, but there's nothing we can do. You'll probably be sort of a glorified errand boy to the brass, and the freighting is going to be heavier than before. They want grapples added to the taxi, so you can figure it out for yourself. Do you still want the job?"

"I came up here to work, sir," Jim answered him. And then his answer startled him. He'd been meaning to ask for Jerry's job; but now that he had it, he had doubts. He'd heard stories of the treatment civilians sometimes got from military officials.

Thorndyke seemed relieved. "Good. I wish I had a hundred men like you. Jim, what are you going to do when this gets finished, if it ever does?"

"I don't know," he admitted. He'd tried to think of an answer, since he'd first swallowed the fact that he could never qualify as a pilot now. "Why, sir?"

Thorndyke played with the papers again, sighing. "Just wondering. I'd hoped . . . Well, there were rumors that we might get another station to build. Television only reaches about a hundred miles now; but if they could get a station twenty-two thousand miles up where it swings around the Earth just once a day—making it stay over the same spot at all times—they'd have a perfect relay station to cover the whole hemisphere. I wanted to recommend you for a job there. But now, if we don't finish this job on schedule . . . Oh, go to bed, Jim. We'll work something out."

The engineer was more worried than Jim had thought. He looked at the production chart on the way out, and scowled. He hadn't known they were that far behind schedule. And with the military work forced on them before they were ready, it would be worse. Something drastic had to be done. Sometimes when a job fell to far behind, a whole crew was fired!

The next day, Jim worked in the machine shop installing the grapples outside the taxi, while the work crews were installing a special lock for the taxi on the hub. It would make it possible for him to drive directly into a shock absorber and open the taxi right into the freight-handling section of the hub. And with the grapples, he could handle freight that would be too big to load inside the little ship.

There was trouble in getting the hub to work right, though. It was supposed to turn on bearings so that motors could cancel its spin while the taxi docked in the lock and unloaded. Then power could be applied to drive back into synchronization with the rest of the station for moving the freight down the tube. But the big bearings had to be put into place exactly, and Dan drove his crew overtime completing the job.

They were barely finished when the rockets began bringing up the military personnel and supplies. They had built four new rockets, and the ships were making two trips a day now. Jim found himself run ragged trying to keep up with it. And his first experience wasn't a pleasant one. A major climbed into the taxi, wheezing from that fat that spelled soft living, and sniffed disdainfully at what he saw.

"Well, I expected to rough it. Young man, I suppose you've been instructed to hold yourself ready for my orders at all times?"

"No, sir," Jim told him.

"Well, you are instructed now. Umm. I think you can begin by taking me around the whole station. I want a good view of my command, naturally."

Jim pointed toward his fuel gauge. "I can't do that, sir. There isn't enough fuel now. Also, I've got a bunch of freight to move. My instructions were to deliver you to the station. Sorry, sir."

Thorndyke fumed when the major went in to have Jim fired. "I have to get that kind of officer, of course! Jim, if you have trouble, report it to me. Your salary is being paid by Major Electric, not by Major Trequil!"

Somehow, though, Jim managed to keep things from coming to a head. He swallowed most of the major's orders, and avoided telling Thorndyke about the others. Most of the personnel arriving to handle the military installations were good men, rigidly tested before they were sent up. And the engineer was having enough trouble in diverting his work forces to rush through completion of the sections occupied by the observatory and guided missile divisions.

Then the bombs came up. Jim had never seen an atomic-armed guided missile, but it took no great genius to guess what they were as he juggled them with the grapples. There seemed to be no end to them. He was getting the hang of jockeying the taxi by then, but it meant long hours of overtime to handle the freight.

It was wonderful progress, he thought bitterly. The science sections waited, while the means for destruction took precedence. He knew it was necessary, since the relations between the United States and the Combine had deteriorated steadily. But the picture of the station as just a vast superfort, while all the things that could enrich the whole Earth waited, wasn't the ideal he'd dreamed of. He knew that Jerry had been a fanatic—and yet this looked very much like what the man had feared.

He wondered about Jerry, briefly. It wouldn't be a death sentence, he was sure, and he was glad of that.

Then the reaction of the Earth to the news that the station was being built came in. Mark brought up a load of the tissue editions of the papers, and Jim dived into them as soon as he was free.

Some of the commentators felt the renewed hope that Jim had once expected. But almost as many were angrily denouncing the government for wasting money that should have gone for more battleships and planes. One came out firmly with the idea that the government had placed the nation in peril by frittering away money on cosmic toys while other nations were building armies.

The letters from the readers filled a whole page. He skipped over the fanatic notes about tampering with What Wasn't Meant to Be. The rest showed confusion. Some wanted to believe, but were unsure of what they could believe; others wanted to disbelieve, and yet somehow clung to the feeling that there was more there than had been announced. It was as if some strange pressure had been relieved while a new one replaced it.

On the international front, things were worse. The Combine had sounded off at once to the World Congress, demanding that action be taken against the United States for building a frightful weapon against all humanity. A number of nations supposedly friendly to the United States had supported the demand.

At the same time, the official press of the Combine began boasting that they had a station planned which could be sent up in sections and assembled before the present one was finished. They claimed flatly that they had rockets driven by atomic power which could haul up immense weights without delay!

It sounded like a wild boast, and yet Jim shuddered. Someday, there would be atomic rockets—at least for all use beyond the atmosphere. If the Combine had developed them . . .

It looked as if the station had only made things worse! Jim tried to stop the doubts, but it was impossible. And he could see the same doubts on the faces of the other men. They were working, but without the drive they would need to have any hopes of finishing in time.

He went out to the taxi for the next load, to find Major Trequil waiting in the lock. "Inspection, Mr. Stanley!" the major announced stiffly. "I'm within my rights! I intend to see how you handle those missiles. I've had complaints!"

Jim shrugged. He was sure there had been no complaints, but he knew there would be after the major finished. But there was nothing to do about that. The man had managed to waste the time of a whole crew while fussing about the exact location of his desk. And the workers were already grumbling about the pampering the military personnel were getting. They had a short-wave radio in their recreation room. The workers didn't have a phonograph.

Jim picked up three men who came out in space suits as the bombs were being shoved out of the evacuated cargo section. He shook his head in annoyance as the major began back-seat driving while he settled the grapples over one. But he managed to catch the bomb snugly, and headed back toward the station.

He was heading along on course when the major jumped up, bobbing against the ceiling of the taxi to stare out of the little bubble top.

"You're high! You're going to miss!" he cried excitedly. "Mr. Stanley, your incompetence—"

"I'm dropping the bomb into the freight lock first," Jim told him. "After that I'll make another pass into the lock and let you out."

"You'll keep me waiting—" the major began indignantly. He let go of the back of the seat to emphasize his point, and began drifting. One of his hands hit the control on the grapple.

The bomb broke free and went headlong along on momentum toward the center of the hub, where it could crash through the wall with its momentum. And the men inside the hub would be working without space suits!

Chapter 14 Decision and Rumor

Men working around the hub began blasting frantically out of the way as the bomb twisted free of the grapples, but Jim had no time to worry about the few when so many were involved. He shoved the yelling major out of the way and began twisting his gyroscope control. The bomb had torn loose from one grapple just as Jim had been making a slight corrective blast, and then had ripped from the other at an angle, slewing sideways.

He didn't dare to miss, or there would be no second chance. And once above it, he had no way to see what the grapples were doing. At the rockets, men had coasted the bomb out into the waiting jaws and signaled when he was to grab. This had to be done by feel.

He waited, holding his breath as the taxi came around over the twisting bomb. Then he hit the grapple controls and felt something catch under him. He couldn't check on how tightly it had been secured. The globe of the hub was already dangerously close. He pushed the wailing gyros to the limit and blasted out with the rocket motor.

There was a wrenching as the force of the rocket began to work against the momentum of the bomb, but the grapples held. Slowly, he began to gain control. The station hub seemed to be touching the taxi, and he tried to coax a gram more of thrust out of the motor.

They shaved within inches of the wall of the hub, but the miss was complete.

He hauled the bomb further out into space, lined it up, and released it. While it was sailing into the lock, he cut around for another pass, and came heading in. The shock basket in front of the lock caught him, and he came to a smooth stop against the seal. Men in the hub snaffled the taxi tight, and threw open the airseals. The major bounced

116

out first, while Jim was turning to give his three other passengers a hand.

"Young man," Major Trequil was shouting, "after this incompetence, you can consider yourself fired. You risked my life with your foolhardy stunting, and I will not tolerate . . ."

Jim swung slowly, pulling off the helmet. He had conquered his temper years before—but he'd also learned that there were times when a man had to stand up for himself. "Major Trequil, you don't hire me, nor do you fire me! And now, if you'll take off your space suit, I've got something that every man in this station wants you to have! Or would you rather admit you're a coward?"

Major Trequil screamed in rage, and began reaching for his zipper, to Jim's surprise. But another voice cut in sharply.

"All right, Jim. That won't solve anything, either." The men from the rocket had pulled off their helmets, and Jim gasped. The speaker was the man who had first interviewed him—Colonel Halpern. He turned to the shocked Major Trequil now.

"I've been hearing reports of your incompetence, Major," he said. "You've confirmed them. You can consider yourself relieved of command here and you will return on the next rocket. I'll have a brief ready to return with you." He saluted and watched while Trequil staggered off. Then he turned to Jim. "I'll expect your co-operation, Jim," he said.

"You'll get it, sir," Jim promised him. The relief of seeing the command shift to a man who knew his business was almost physical. He was sure that Halpern was competent.

The change in command helped the station morale somewhat. But it was deteriorating too fast for anything to repair it. There was a fight in the kitchen, and the hazing of the new men grew vicious. Most of the tension was coming from their uncertainty, but it centered on Earth. Normally, Thorndyke was a good boss. But he wasn't able to handle this situation. Work fell further behind. Jim kept an eye on

117

the production chart, and grew sicker as the schedule fell further and further behind.

The presence of the military personnel alone was a source of trouble. The men behaved well, but they were a constant reminder to the station gang that other men would take over the work they did. And there seemed to be no future for them below.

Jim wished now that the news of the station had never been released. Nations began to pull away from their solidarity with the Alliance in the debates at the World Congress. They had studied the orbit of the station and found that during its two-hour circle around the Earth, it passed over nearly every country, and had a clear view far beyond its actual passage.

Rumors of other stations grew wilder, with one South American nation even claiming they had a station built on the ground which would be sent up in a single piece. It was impossible, since no rocket that big could be built—it would have covered half the globe; and no station light enough for even such a rocket would be strong enough to stand the terrific acceleration. But some of the men in the station believed it until Thorndyke finally managed to convince them. Then the rumor that the Combine had guided missiles ready to send against the station gained favor.

When the men, with full information available, could believe such things, it was no wonder that the people below were becoming panicky. The unemployment figures were going up, adding to the trouble. Apparently the government was counting on the station, and cutting back on its other projects.

That meant that the men here would have even less future, once the station was done. If they had been up to schedule, and if the television industry had decided to build the second station, there would have been something to hope for. But now that seemed to have been abandoned.

Jim's worries about his future had increased. He would have money waiting for him, but it wouldn't last forever. Aside from his space work, he had little experience that would get him a decent job. He still wanted to finish his education, but he had no idea of what to specialize in, now that rocketry was out.

Nora caught him in the hall while he was brooding, and dragged him to the newly finished recreation room. "You haven't dropped in to see me for a week, Jim," she protested. "You can't bury yourself in your shell, at least not all the time."

He tried to laugh it off, but ended by spilling all his worries to her. It felt good to get them off his chest, and Nora was a good listener.

She sighed, when he finished. "It's too bad we don't have more men like Bart," she decided. "He kept the men from thinking too much about things they couldn't help. Mr. Bailey knows his business, but he keeps to himself too much, too. And you're even worse. Jim, the men think a lot of you. You could do a lot to help. But there's nobody here to lead them."

Bart's words came into his mind. He finally left Nora and started toward his quarters, trying to figure it out. He'd meant to follow Bart's advice, but instead he'd turned into even more of a lone wolf. He knew it was wrong, but he had no idea of what to do about it.

Abruptly, he swung around and headed for the cabin Terrence shared with another man. He found the little man sitting over a clipping from one of the papers, staring at it lugubriously. It was an account of how the Cuban Government had protested the building of the space station without consultation among friendly nations.

Jim dropped into the opposite bunk. "Forget it, Terrence. Cuba isn't unique. About half of our own government is condemning the other half for starting this."

Terrence shook his head. "Maybe." Then he stared at Jim, studying his face. "Jim, you don't look good. You've been killing yourself. How about a game of darts?"

They went up to the recreation room. There was only a small group of men there, though it should have been the gathering place for all of them when they were off. Most of them just sat talking listlessly. It seemed impossible that things had gone so much awry.

A short, fat little man came up as they started to play and stood watching. He was obviously bored and disgusted, and Jim invited him to join them, introducing himself and Terrence.

"Phil Ross," the other acknowledged. "The most wasted biologist on record."

It turned out that he'd been sent up to install a new air system, just before the military needs had taken up everyone's time on the station. Tanks and cans of frozen algae had been sent up ahead, and were piled in a dump a mile away. He'd been trying to get the use of a crew of men and the taxi to make the installation, but so far all he'd got was Thorndyke's sympathy.

"It's ridiculous, too," he added, aiming at the target and missing as he threw too hard. "It takes three pounds of oxygen plus containers for every man here each day. That's a lot of weight to ferry up from Earth. And it's pure waste. Three square feet of algae in water an inch deep will supply enough air for one man—and do it permanently, by breaking down the carbon dioxide to release the oxygen. The plumbing is in, there's space for my project, and all the supplies. So nothing happens."

Jim considered it. Here was work that needed doing badly, while he'd been trying to find some means of speeding things up. Bart would have got it done, he was sure. And abruptly, Jim decided that this was his test.

Thorndyke gave him permission to use the taxi without bothering to ask his purpose. He let Terrence in on his plans, and they went around contacting the gang who had worked under Bart. The idea of getting the old gang together offered enough interest for them to accept, and they all appeared after work in a corner of the recreation room. And for a while the conversation was animated. Then it lagged, while Jim tried to think of a way to sell them his idea.

"Three more girls came up the last trip," one of them announced during one of the lulls. "We ought to get a radio or a phonograph. Throw a dance! The guys over in military have a radio."

Abruptly, Jim saw the angle he'd been looking for. He could almost hear Bart's words in his head. He nodded. "They've got everything. And we can't even get fresh air because we're too busy on their projects." He told them about Ross and the air system, making it sound as simple and glamorous as he could.

One of the men reacted as Jim had hoped. "Yeah, it's like them. The regular men and noncoms ain't so bad. But the graft they pull . . ."

"For two cents," Terrence cut in quickly, picking up the lead, "I'd show them a thing or two. Man, I'm tired of smelling generator oil just to keep them in style. Hey, I wonder if that fresh air would actually work?"

He raised his voice. Phil Ross had been sitting at the opposite end of the hall, and now he came over. It took half an hour of tossing it around, but in the end the men got up and began putting on their suits. Jim went for the taxi, and came back to find Nora also dressed to help, daring him by her looks to send her back. But he felt too good over his victory.

There was plenty to do. That part of the station was still unfinished. Huge windows of heavy plastic had to be installed to let in the sunlight, and equipped with shutters to regulate the amount. The inner walls had to be put up, and the whole made airtight. There were the tanks to be coupled to the plumbing, and blowers to be connected to the air ducts. Jim lugged the supplies in the taxi, saving time by dropping them through the open walls of the section. It made it hard work to match speed with the rotating station and hold the taxi in a circular orbit, but it took care of the handling easily.

They hardly made a dent in the job during the four hours they worked the first night, and Jim had visions of the men giving up before any real progress could show.

Congress took care of that for him. A bill was introduced by one of the representatives to take over the station and build it with Army personnel. He made it sound attractive as a way of saving time and money, and it took fast work on the part of the opposing side to get the bill voted down by the narrow margin of two votes.

Jim was pretty sure that the Army didn't want the job, and he knew that Halpern had fumed when he read of it. But the rumor had spread through the station that the military branches were trying to get Congress to kick out the workers and let the Army take over. The next evening there was a bigger turnout for work.

It took the men only four days altogether to complete the job, and at the end over half the working force of the station was busy on it, using their own time without grumbling. It felt like the first days of the station. And Jim had noticed that it hadn't hurt the rest of the work. The men who worked nights kidded the others about being lazy, and then had to pitch in on their regular jobs to keep up with the men they'd been ribbing—until it was a contest between the overtime and the non-overtime workers.

Jim had been doubtful of the algae's ability to function after being frozen solid for the trip; but the green stuff in the tanks began to form little bubbles after Ross's treatment of it. It wasn't the freshest air in the world, but it was better than the canned stuff. And when they cut off the oxygen bottles, there was no loss of breathability.

They would still need oxygen bottles for a reserve, but the big shipment was no longer necessary. As they broke up, Jim wondered whether he could get Thorndyke to have some small luxuries sent up. They wouldn't weigh as much as the oxygen, and they'd help keep the men happy.

Thorndyke shook his head. "Not until the military stock pile is complete, Jim. Come on back here, I want to talk to you."

He lead the way past the desks of the other engineers into his small private office.

"I appreciate what you did on that air plant," he said. He smiled for a second. Sure, I knew all about it, and we needed the work, too. But don't plan on any more like it. For one thing, it won't work. The men liked the game—but the next time, it will be work, not fun. They catch on. For another, we can't risk any serious bad relations with the military personnel here. Stop and think a minute. Nora tells me you keep trying to do what Bart would have done. But did Bart ever stir up any hatred?"

"No, sir." There'd been the kidding of the college men, but that had been in front of their faces, and they'd soon discovered it was just a running gag. "I didn't want to start any hatred."

"And it didn't, this time. Or nothing that's serious. Colonel Halpern's informed Earth his men need two radios, and he's going to lend one to our recreation hall. That should patch up any hard feeling. But if you drove the point home harder—as you'd have to next time—it would wind up in enmity between the two groups."

Jim stood up to go. Thorndyke motioned him back to the seat. "One thing more. Dan Bailey's quitting, and he has asked me to put you in as foreman in his place. But—"

"Dan's quitting?" It shocked Jim. He'd counted on Dan to the bitter end. "Why?"

Thorndyke sighed. "You ask him. I tried to find out why. But he's been here over six months, so he has the right. Anyhow, Jim, what I wanted to say was that I don't think you're ready to be a foreman yet. You're probably the best man I have—no, I mean that—but even though the men have a lot of respect for you, I don't think you're close enough to them. Besides, I need a good taxi jockey. So I'm making Terrence Rodriguez foreman. Okay?"

"Okay—and you've got a good man," Jim said. He shoved up from his chair and headed back to his own cabin.

He'd tried to do what Bart had asked, and he'd thought he was succeeding. Instead, he'd only been kidding himself.

Chapter 15

Dan couldn't be shaken from his decision. "I'm going to marry one of the girls who first came up here—Marge Whitely," he explained to Jim. "And there's no future in this. The work isn't getting done. When the time is up and the penalty clause is put into effect, every foreman here will have a black mark against him. Or maybe Major Electric will fire the whole crew tomorrow, the way things are going. I'm going back and handle the coupling of the rocket stages."

Jim hadn't even known that Dan was interested in one of the girls, though they had been roommates for weeks now. No wonder Thorndyke didn't think he was close enough to the men. He told the foreman of the conversation.

Dan shrugged. "Thorndyke doesn't know how to handle men himself. He should have followed through when you got them stirred up. But don't think Bart could have done it, either. You've got to stop making a hero of Bart. He was a great guy. But when he was here, we had a small group and everybody was happy being here. He gave you some good advice about getting to know people, and you'll feel better if you follow it. But stop trying to be someone else, boy!"

The next day Jim took him and a rather plain, pleasant girl out to the rocket that was to carry him back to Earth. He'd tried to think of some fancy speech for farewell, but he finally stuck out his hand. "Going to miss you, Dan!"

The older man nodded, gulping. "See you, boy!" Then the rocket swallowed him, and Jim had to head back for the station, wondering for the hundredth time if he shouldn't have gone along while the going was good.

The radio arrived from Colonel Halpern in time for them to hear the end of the debate at the World Congress.

Jim had wondered what would come of it. The small nations wanted all stations outlawed; the Combine wanted the United States condemned and forced to wait until another station could be built; and a few idealists wanted the space station taken over by the World Congress to put teeth into world government. Nobody had enough votes to pass a proposal, and after a long huddle, they came up with what they called a compromise.

The ruling was that space was not a national affair. There was no statement that it was an international affair, however. The Combine claimed a victory and blasted the United States for using the station for national purposes in space. The United States claimed a similar victory, pointing to the fact that the sea was not a national affair, but that ships on it served national ends. Boiled down, the decision had said exactly nothing.

Jim went away sick. The men doing the debating had never seen a space station. They'd never looked down on the Earth from a height of a thousand miles and seen what an easy target it would be. They didn't spend their time moving over national boundaries until nations blurred together.

In irresponsible hands, the station could be used to make slaves of the rest of the world. In the right hands, it could make war impossible by flatly warning the nations that the first act of war would lead to extermination of all military centers. But even then, while the nations were learning that, the results could be horrible.

So long as some peoples could be made to believe in the same old ways and hates, there was no safety, even from the station. It would do little good to bomb the Combine, if the Combine first dropped fifty hydrogen bombs on the cities of the United States. The station might end the war, but it would be a victory little better than death.

Jim had dreamed of a station which could help the whole world. Accurate weather predictions for weeks ahead would save billions from damage to crops and property. With the conditions of space in which to work, science might move ahead by long leaps. Astronomy would enter a new era when there was no thick blanket of air to make their pictures fuzzy and unclear. And men could go on to other planets.

The only use for the station being discussed now was its military value. Everything had to wait for the bombs. And the men on the station had no inspiration beyond fear to make them work.

The next day the radio brought the news that the Combine had developed an atomic rocket and atomic guided missiles. Details were to be announced to the world within the next few days.

It was Halpern's face, when he went to confer with Thorndyke, that gave the first indication that this was more than a boast. The flat promise of details must have taken it out of the usual propaganda class.

Nora shook her head suddenly, and called Jim over to a group who were discussing it. "Jim, isn't the station safe from all guided missiles?"

He wanted to lie to them, to tell them they were in no danger. But he knew that word would get out sooner or later.

"From most guided missiles," he answered. "They'd have to be almost the size of the rocket ships, and we could get our own missiles out to intercept them. We're a small target and hard to hit, if the enemy has only a few bombs. But with atomic-powered rockets—I don't know. They could accelerate a lot longer, probably, so that they'd arrive at a terrific speed. And they'd be smaller, harder to spot in time, and cheaper—which means more could be used."

It was the first time there had been any reason to think that they might be in personal danger up here. But once they could be reached, they'd be the first target of any nation wanting to make war.

Eight men quit their jobs that night, and nothing Thorndyke could do would make them stay. Work slowed down even further.

The Combine lived up to its word this time. Two days

later Mark brought up the papers, and the front pages carried the details on the new Combine developments.

There were diagrams and scientific formulae. It was nothing like the usual propaganda release. In fact, there were no absurd claims. They simply stated what they had, listing the ability of the new ship. The figures were incredible to anyone who was used to the three-stage chemical rockets. But with power from the atom, those figures could very well be true.

There were even plans for the rocket ship, and Jim pored over them. Usually an artist's drawing of a future development has everything too orthodox and similar to everything else, or too completely new. These drawings looked like the real thing. The construction of the rocket nozzle was unlike any Jim had ever seen—but it looked practical. Some of the framing of the actual rocket showed that it had been designed by someone who had calculated the stresses and strains carefully, and built to fit them.

The scientists on Earth were being cautious. Of course, the material released wasn't complete—it held back a number of facts which would be needed for the building of such a ship, as was to be expected. But nothing that was stated or claimed was impossible, though it would seem to be quite advanced.

There was no one on the station who was an expert on atomic power, since none was used in space, due to its need for heavy, massive shielding. Thorndyke was the best man they could find to ask.

"How about it, Mr. Thorndyke?" one of the men called out to him as he came out of the military section. "How much of this is propaganda? What are they doing—trying to scare us long enough for them to work up some dirty trick? I've seen this big secret stuff of theirs before."

"It's too early to be sure, but it looks as if they have something. Maybe they've exaggerated the figures a little, though." Thorndyke grinned at the man, and went on into his office, leaving some relief behind him. Everyone had a clear idea of how much the Combine could exaggerate.

But Jim found Thorndyke with his head on his hands,

staring at the charts and diagrams in the paper with eyes red from lack of sleep and from worry. There was no smile now. He nodded to Jim. "This time, I guess they've got it —maybe even that sectional station they were talking about. It could be built up a lot faster on the ground, and with atomic power they might be able to haul up such sections. They've been boasting they can have a station up before we finish. Maybe they càn."

"Then we'd better get our station in working order first, and hope they don't have quite all they claim," Jim said. He'd tried to sound hopeful, but the doubt crept into his voice before he could finish.

Thorndyke sighed, and looked at the production chart. "I don't know. Sometimes I think we're licked."

"How about putting on more men to rush the job?"

"We've got all we can. And now those who can are quitting. We'll probably lose them faster than we can find volunteers who will pass the tests." The engineer sighed. "Jonas is in Washington now, trying to get them to extend our time limit."

Even Nora was beginning to lose faith. "My grandfather was a doctor," she told Jim. "An old style one. He drove a horse and buggy when all the others were using cars. And when they were building a fine new hospital in our town, Granddad had to sell the horse to pay his taxes. Nobody wanted the buggy. There's no use trying to keep on with old ideas if someone has something better."

Jim wavered then. But a stubborn streak in him held out. And now he was beginning to know some of the men. He had started to hang around their groups in the background, trying to find from their talk why the work was so slow. It was soon obvious that none of them knew. As far as they could tell, they were working harder than before, even though they were accomplishing less. But since Jim had studied some rocketry, he was the nearest thing to an authority they had, and he was drawn into their conversations. Somehow, knowing them by name didn't seem to make him much closer, though.

All he could learn was that they were worried about

staying on the station where any day might bring an atomic guided missile and even more worried about going back to Earth where things were happening that they couldn't understand at all.

"If the Combine planned this to keep us from finishing," he told Nora, "they did a good job of it."

But it wasn't all propaganda. Ten days later, the Combine announced that their new rocket had taken off for an orbit around Earth. The report cut into a program of light music, a translation of the official report.

"We interrupt this program to bring you an important announcement," the announcer began in routine words, but with a shocked voice. "At eleven P.M., New York time, a one-stage atomic rocket lifted from the airfield outside the Combine capital, carrying three men. It is reported to have a total weight of four hundred tons, of which less than two tons are fuel. The ship took off in an easterly direction, after rising to a height of nearly thirty miles. Some observers report that it reached an acceleration of twice that of any other rocket, though this seems unlikely, since acceleration is limited by the ability of the human body to take such strain. Neutral observers who were present by invitation of the Combine report that there can be no question but that it was an atomic-powered ship, however . . ."

Thorndyke stepped into the room and stopped, staring at the radio. From the military section, Colonel Halpern came running toward them. He stared at the blasting radio, and nodded. He was stunned.

"So you heard it," he said. "It's true. We had confirmation from one of our own rockets that was coming in on a landing! One stage! They must have had it when they first announced it!"

Men were streaming into the recreation room as the word was spread throughout the station. A group of men from the outside hadn't even removed their helmets.

Halpern turned back to his own quarters. "If your place is too small, send any who want to come over to us. There's no secrecy up here any more, anyhow."

A few of the men filed after him, and more left as the last of the workers forced their way into the crowded room.

Jim still couldn't believe it. Neither of the two known atomic reactions was suitable. The bomb let loose a terrific force, but so quickly that it could shatter its container before giving thrust; the atomic pile gave out a steady stream of energy which could be controlled, but, for its weight, any of the chemical explosives was capable of more thrust.

Even the ideal of all fuel combinations, the theoretically perfect mixture of fluorine and beryllium, however, couldn't deliver the thrust that the ship being described had developed. It had to be a true atomic rocket.

"Naval radar stations have detected the flight of the Combine rocket over the Western Coastal waters of the United States," the radio announced. "From a hasty plotting of its path, it seems that it intends to take up an orbit 180 degrees behind our own station—in the same orbit, but on the other side of the Earth."

A few of the listeners looked disappointed. Most of them seemed relieved. Obviously there was much more fear of the Combine rocket than there was curiosity about it.

Thorndyke spotted the fear and shook his head. "There's no danger from this rocket," he told them. "It's a demonstration, not a military attack on us. You're all perfectly safe. And if there ever is any danger, you'll be shipped to Earth at the first sign."

"If I'm going to die, I'd rather die right here," one of the men shouted. There was a sudden murmur of agreement and countermutter of disagreement.

A few more reports came in to indicate that the path of the rocket was being followed. Once its general path was known, and radar stations were alerted, a few of the bigger installations could locate it. The first estimate of its path seemed to be completely correct. It was rising on an ascent that would put it at the same height as the station.

"We've had an eyewitness account through neutral channels," the radio piped up. "One added feature emerges. The Combine rocket had small steering vanes, but no gliding wings. It must depend on the full use of its rocket power to descend, without using a gliding approach."

It was like saying that they had so much power they enjoyed wasting it. To come down on rocket power took the same amount of power as going up.

Then abruptly there was a sharp, shocked sound from the radio, followed by a second of silence. When the voice sounded again, it was incredulous, loud, and as slow-spoken as a man coming out of a deep sleep.

"Attention! Attention! Word has just been received that the Combine rocket exploded forty seconds after achieving a stable orbit. Repeat, the Combine rocket has exploded. The Combine radio has gone off the air, but the explosion was clearly seen by a telescope observer, whose position fix agrees with all predictions of the path of the rocket. The Combine rocket has exploded."

Chapter 16 Castaways from Earth

There was stunned silence in the station. Jim gazed around, seeing some faces showing relief while others held the shock normal to news of any catastrophe. He himself was numbed from the strain and the final announcement. The words that still came babbling out of the radio meant nothing to him. He dropped into a seat as another man got up excitedly, staring at the lighted dial, but hardly hearing the sounds from the speaker.

He felt someone shaking his shoulder and looked around in annoyance. Mark Emmett was standing behind him, his space suit helmet shoved back, staring at the crowd.

"What's going on here?" he asked. "Nobody brings me the taxi out when I orbit in, there's nobody in the hub—and now you act as if the world just blew up! Hey, don't tell me that war—"

"Not quite," Jim answered. He filled in the facts as quickly as he could while Mark squeezed in beside him. The radio began repeating the news, and Jim kept quiet for Mark to listen.

The pilot shook his head to clear it. "I saw them rushing around on the field just before I took off. But I didn't know a thing about it."

Thorndyke leaned forward, turning the volume up suddenly. The announcer's voice had lost its drone of repetition, and was calling, demanding attention.

". . . a radio appeal to the United States, claiming the men on the exploded rocket are still alive. This unprecedented action has caused a furor in the World Congress, where the Combine delegate was caught in the middle of an accusation of the United States as party responsible for the blowup of the ship. Here is the radio message:

" 'To the Government of the United States of America! The Combined People's States of Europe and Asia have

132

received a distress signal from the rocket which so unfortunately exploded while setting new records for science. This indicates that the men aboard are still alive. Among these men is the illustrious younger nephew of our glorious leader, whose work with rocket-propelled planes and short-range rockets has made his renown universal. In the name of the brotherhood of humanity, the Combined People's States ask the assistance of the United States of America in the rescue of these brave heroes!'

"The government is reported to be readying a reply, indicating everything will be done to save the men. This will be announced as soon as it is released. Meantime . . ."

Jim frowned. The "illustrious younger nephew" must be Peter Chiam, the number one choice to succeed the ruler, who really had established records with his rocket work. The Combine must have been absolutely sure of success to let him go on the ship.

He heard the announcer say something about the Combine estimating that there were oxygen supplies for only six more hours on the ship, and felt Mark suddenly stiffen.

"The other rockets on the field won't be ready by then! They don't have one assembled yet. It'll take them eight hour to get ready. Jim, how much fuel do you have stored here for the taxi?"

"Several tons. Mark! Do you think you can do it from here?"

"Why bother?" someone yelled. "Let 'em die! They——"

He was booed down at once. A lot of the men could remember what it felt like to be castaways from Earth, with their oxygen running out. Combine men or not, the crew of the wrecked ship were human beings.

Mark was figuring a rough orbit. He'd have to take off upward from the station orbit, adding speed to carry him well out into space, until the pull of the Earth could pull the ship back to the orbit he'd left. It would take the Combine wreck two hours to swing around and back to the other side of the Earth. He would have to swing out far enough to make up the difference between that and the single hour it would take the station to reach the same spot.

133

The return would be the same, to bring them back where they had started.

He threw the paper to Jim. "It may work. You get the men in the bombsighting section to figure this out, Jim, while I get the rocket ready. And get ready to come along, if this works. I'll need someone who's used to juggling a ship the way you handle the taxi, in case anything goes wrong. Game?"

For a chance at the rocket controls, Jim would have gone if the chance had been only one in a million. But the uniformed men in the bombing division fed the necessary information into their computers and began solving for the closest approximation without much doubt of the possibility. The final orbit and fuel figures indicated it was going to be close, but there was some margin for error. Colonel Halpern ordered the news transmitted to Earth, and Jim rushed out to begin taxiing the extra fuel to the men working on the rocket tanks.

Nora came out in her suit at the last minute, bringing three space suits for the stranded men and emergency equipment to take care of them until they could be returned. Dr. Perez, it seemed, had decided that his place was in the station dispensary, and that Nora was more suited to the trip.

Jim settled into the copilot's seat while Mark fed the orbit figures to the automatic pilot and gave him a last-second briefing. "You'll handle all the juggling around we may have to do where we have to fly by feel, and I'll handle the piloting on the regular orbit. The controls are the same as those on your taxi, if you forget the ones you won't need. It's bigger, but the same amount of acceleration and turnover will get the same results. Okay, up ship!"

The automatic pilot cut on the rockets for long seconds at reasonable acceleration, and then cut them off. On the screen, the station seemed to drop below them and begin moving ahead. They were making greater speed now, but moving out where the circle around Earth was much longer. The station continued to forge slowly ahead.

After that, it was a long period of waiting while they

rose slowly, losing speed, and then began to turn under the force of Earth's gravity, to fall back toward the orbit of the station. They would touch it exactly two hours after their start, making this the longest flight ever attempted. Jim spent the time getting the feel of the larger controls. He'd at least be able to say that he'd served a hitch as a rocket man!

The clicking of the automatic pilot was the first sure sign that they were nearing their objective. The ship had turned over automatically, and now the rockets blasted out, to bring them back to the same speed and orbit as the station, but an hour behind it.

They stared into the screens, looking for a sign of the wreck. At first there was nothing but empty space. Then something seemed to slide over a star. They stared at it, while the radar reached out and pin-pointed it. There was only one pip showing on the screen. Mark lifted his hands from the controls. "Take over!"

Jim's hands were sweating. The wreckage was about twenty miles away, and at a slightly different speed and direction. He had to match course with it while using the minimum amount of fuel. And there was no way of figuring it out accurately on the piloting computers here.

He tried to get the feel of it in his head. He'd long since reached the point where the taxi was under his automatic control. But convincing himself that the big rocket would work the same way over such a distance was rough work. His hands were sweating as he finally reached out to cut on a gentle blast, after turning the ship slightly on its gyroscopes. It felt right to him, and he had to assume that it was right. He began turning on the gyroscopes as they drifted toward the wreck.

Finally, when it felt right to him, he used a counterblast to cut their speed. His eyes froze on the screen that showed the wreck, while his body collapsed in the contour seat.

Mark sighed, showing that his confidence hadn't been as great as he had pretended. "Good work, Jim. You didn't freeze. We're three hundred feet off side, and holding steady enough. Okay, let's get over there."

They slipped into their suits. Nora gathered up her equipment, and the two men took the extra suits. They let the pumps evacuate the cargo space. It would be simpler to leave the lock completely open for their return, rather than trying to carry men who might be wounded through the narrow space, one door at a time.

What was left of the Combine ship was a dull, burnt cinder of metal, with one edge indicating that it had been built to break free from the power section at the first sign of explosion. The control cabin must have been freed before the explosion, in fact, since it hadn't been completely wrecked in the atomic flare-up. In the vacuum of space, any blast carried much less violence than it did where air could transmit the shock. Still, they must have had warning and been free sometime before the power section blew itself into invisible dust.

They jumped off with the sureness of experience, to land on the strange air lock. There was a lever there, and Mark pulled it. Immediately, a section like the breechblock of a gun spun part way around and turned outward. Inside the lock, they watched it close automatically, while air rushed in. Then the inner door swung open by itself.

There was good design here—and the luxury of automatic controls that were possible when there was no limit to the amount of weight their blast could lift.

Three men were stretched out on seats that seemed to be made of thin plastic filled with some yielding liquid, and at first glance they all seemed to be dead. Then the youngest one stirred, opening his eyes and staring at them. Jim bent down, not expecting to understand.

But the words were in English. "Thanks, Yanks. Knew you'd come. Been hanging on, waiting. I'm Peter Chiam, and they—they . . ."

He fell back, panting, his eyes closed.

"Shock," Nora said, and began working with a hypodermic, while Jim and Mark started to pull the space suits over the other two. She turned to them, making a quick examination while they put a suit on Chiam. She was frowning when they turned back.

"This one seems to be all right," she said. "But the big man—there's no sign of breath or pulse."

Jim felt for the wrist, and then put his ear to the man's chest. The skin was slightly cooler than his face, and there was no sound. He stood up, straightening out the arms.

Mark scurried around the cabin for a few seconds, studying the strange machines that had controlled the ship. Then he reached for the smaller man, while Jim lifted Chiam into his arms. They said nothing about the other, and made no effort to remove the space suit. Where every ounce might count against their tiny reserve of fuel, they could not afford to be sentimental about returning a body to its people.

The lock let them through automatically again, the inner seal clanging shut quickly, and the outer seal closing after them. They kicked off into space, heading to their own lock. Inside their rocket, they placed the two injured and drugged men onto the extra contour seats and strapped them down.

Nora was still working on the men, and Mark settled into his seat, drawing a small notebook from the pouch of his folded space suit. "A souvenir," he said, and there was a faint reddening of his face. "One of the men was doodling all during the flight, as well as making notes. It's full of formulae and idle jottings, as well as of their unreadable script. Maybe our scientists can make something of it."

He sounded apologetic. Jim grimaced. The idea of looting the wreck wasn't one he cared for. Yet he knew he'd have picked it up, too, if he'd spotted it. Ethics were twisted things in a world where men's relations with each other were getting steadily worse.

Nora came back to her seat and began buckling in, keeping an eye on her charges. Mark sighed, and reached for the button on the automatic pilot.

Then Jim shouted. It had been only a trace of movement on one of the screens, seen out of the corner of his eye. But it had come where no movement could be. He swung his head, hunting for it again. Then he pointed. "Mark! The lock—the lock on the Combine ship is open!"

It might have been some fault with the automatic controls of the lock. But Jim and Mark came to their feet at once. Jim reached his suit and was into it first, from greater experience. Mark dropped back to the pilot seat, letting him go. He forced his way through the air lock, cursing the slowness of the device. Then he was sailing across to the open lock of the Combine wreck.

The air had rushed from the control cabin, since both doors of the lock had been opened at once. He twisted through them, and into the cabin.

The man who had been left for dead was staring at him out of the vision plate of the sealed helmet. He had pulled himself up until one arm rested on a control panel, and his finger was still stretched out onto the button that must have controlled the lock. His eyes were wide open, staring at Jim with horror in them.

Then they relaxed, and he sank slowly into himself.

Jim lifted him easily in the weightlessness and felt a sob go through the man's body. It must have been a horrible experience to waken and find the others gone, to find himself deserted here, and not even to know whether the rescue ship was near enough to summon again. He'd kept his wits, however. He'd given the only signal he could, without faltering, and then had somehow hung on, not daring to hope until he saw Jim's figure come through the lock.

Jim put him onto the final chair in the rocket, and Nora went to him, using the hypo again. Out of the helmet, the man's face was strained and ghastly white. But he smiled faintly at the prick of the needle. "We thought you were dead!" Nora gasped.

He nodded weakly. "I, too, gracious lady!"

Nora avoided their eyes, but Mark reached a hand out as she sank to her chair. "Jim thought he was dead, too, girl. Forget it. We've all heard of shock producing a coma that even the best doctors have mistaken for death. Anyhow, he's safe."

He gave her no time for an answer as he hit the button and the rocket blasted off again, lifting into its arching orbit that would bring them back near the space station.

The rescued men slept on under the drug, and Nora began using plasma on them to counteract the shock effects as the ship sped on.

Finally the rocket went on again, while Jim and Mark searched for the space station. When the blast cut off, it lay less than three miles away. The errors in the hastily computed orbit must have been partly canceled out by the maneuvering to reach the wreck.

Jim touched the controls, wondering how much fuel was left. He blasted, turned over and waited. But there was enough fuel to bring them to a stop.

He sat with the controls in his hands while Dr. Perez and others came out to them, knowing that when he let go, his career as a pilot would be over. Then, sighing, he stood up to help carry the men into the station.

Chapter 17

For a few days, Jim and Mark had been heroes. But at the end of a week they had been forgotten on the front pages of the papers. Jim was glad when the shouting was over.

The three rescued men had pulled through, and were already back in Combine territory. The fancy medals that the three on the rescue party had received from the Combine had been stored away on Earth, forgotten.

The notebook had never been mentioned publicly. But Jim had been told enough to satisfy most of his curiosity when the scientists had finished going over it. The Combine method of getting slow hydrogen fission was one that had been suggested before, but never tried; and decision to use it had been caused by a hidden error that had given misleading results to their whole attack on it. It was a minor miracle that the explosion had taken so long.

Yet in the notebook had been other formulae and equations that opened up new possibilities, when coupled with the knowledge the scientists already had. The Combine had developed side trails on atomics, and the combination of those and what was already known might lead to true atomic-powered space flight someday—twenty years or so in the future.

After that, there were only unpleasant repercussions. A man on one of the appropriations subcommittees in Congress began a series of systematic attacks on the way the station was being built, suggesting slyly that it was behind schedule because men were wasting their time and the tax-payers' money on romantic publicity tricks. Papers that had cheered wildly a few days before thought it over and decided that there was a lot of truth in the speech.

It didn't help when an announcement came out that Peter Chiam's wife had given birth to twins shortly after his return, and that they were named James and Mark.

There were strange attempts at humor then about the rarefied atmosphere of our good relations with the Combine. The paper with the largest circulation ran a lead cartoon with a thermometer marked "warm above 1000, freezing below." It was reprinted widely.

Jim came in from ferrying in the last of the military equipment. That one section of the station was now completed. He went into Thorndyke's office to give him the official mail that had come out on the rocket.

Thorndyke motioned him into a seat, and began tearing the letters open, skimming them. He threw one across the desk, where Jim could see it. "That kills that. Our appeal to have the date for completion delayed was denied. It looks as if we're going to be held to our penalty clause."

"What is this penalty clause?" Jim asked. He'd heard about it for months, but it had never been explained.

Thorndyke leaned back wearily. "A result of my own bad estimate, I guess. I went over the plans when the government secretly asked for bids on the station, and I estimated we could do it in nine months. So our bid carried a time limit of one year. And they insisted on a penalty clause if it couldn't be finished by then. Under that, if it's not completed by the end of the year, the entire station reverts to the government at that time, and the government can then hire anyone it chooses to finish the project, at the expense of Major Electric, plus a fine for each day for the inconvenience caused. It isn't such an unusual arrangement. But whoever completes the station won't worry about expenses. It won't drive Major Electric bankrupt—but it will hurt more than any company can afford to take. Darn it, I told them I was an engineer, not a supervisor. But they insisted on sending me out here!"

Thorndyke went back to his brooding, while Jim turned to the production chart. At the beginning, they had done better than had been expected, even though they had been shorthanded. But now they had four months' work left to do, and less than two in which to do it. He couldn't see any way of finishing on time.

"Jonas is coming out!" Thorndyke said suddenly. He

twisted his mouth bitterly, and shoved the papers away. "He's the head of this whole project, and one of the four big shots in Major Electric."

"I've met him," Jim admitted, remembering the man who'd first interviewed him for the job. "He didn't seem to be a dragon."

"He isn't—but he's the man who makes the decisions when things go wrong. I knew they meant to send out someone to check up on the work here—they've had engineers up here for the last three months making suggestions. But Jonas! What it means, Jim, is that the company is trying to make up its mind whether to dump the project now and try to get some easement on the penalty, or whether it's cheaper to go ahead and try to force it as near completion as possible."

"You mean, they can fire us all," Jim said. He'd wondered at times why the company hadn't started general firings in a last-ditch effort to get things humming again. But it had never been close to reality.

"Not without paying you for the full time," Thorndyke said.

Jim remembered that the contract held certain guarantees. He had read it quickly at the time, and he could only dimly recall something about payment for six months during any period where a certain minimum time was spent on the station. So there would be no loss of money. But it wasn't a very cheering thought.

Jonas came up two days later, still looking like a gray-haired, kindly businessman at his club. He went over production charts and into the sections where the work was incomplete. The men stared at him angrily, but he disregarded their glares. He had interviewed most of them and remembered their names and the way they had taken the interviews. And slowly, he began to meet with smiles wherever he went.

The station rumor was that everything was going to be all right, now that Jonas had come. But Jim had seen the sharpness with which the man had studied the slacking work, and the piles of figures that he was working over.

Thorndyke was a sick man. He looked very haggard, and his eyes followed Jonas as if expecting an ax to fall on his neck at any minute.

The third day after Jonas came, Jim found the engineer going through his desk, pulling out the few things there, and putting them into a small bag. He came to an abrupt halt, and Thorndyke looked up, smiling for the first time in days.

"I've been canned, Jim," he said simply. "I'm being shipped back to Earth, where Jonas tells me my talents will be of greater service to the company. He's taking over until he can make up his mind."

"We'll strike!" Jim began hotly. "He can't do that!"

Thorndyke shrugged. "He certainly can, Jim. If he hadn't had such a tough wrestle in Washington to keep things from being worse, he'd have done it a long time ago, I guess. And darn it, he's right. I'm no good at this job."

Jim knew there was some truth to it. Thorndyke had been all right at first—and if the outside pressures hadn't ruined morale, or if he'd had a subordinate who could take off some of the strain, he might have pulled off the contract safely. He wasn't a good man for the job now. But he'd treated them well, and they couldn't just let him take the rap for them.

"We'll strike!" he repeated.

Thorndyke laughed bitterly. "Who'll strike, Jim? Haven't you heard from the men what a great guy Jonas is? He has them eating out of his hand. That's why he's an executive. Besides, I don't want anyone striking. This was my baby, and I still want to see it finished. If Thorndyke can't do it, let's hope that Jonas can."

Then he stood looking around the halls and the work that had been finished. Finally he picked up his bag. "I'll be back here sometime, Jim. But now, the sooner you can get me to the rocket, the better."

The men took Jonas' statement that Thorndyke had been suffering from overwork and had been sent back to rest up without a question. They had liked Thorndyke, but had

143

never given him the loyalty that they seemed to give the new man.

Jonas sensed Jim's reaction at once, and smiled as he was passing in the hallway. "I like to see a young man who is loyal to his boss, Jim," he said. "Go ahead and hate me. But I warn you, if you keep it up, I'm just mean enough to use that hate for my own purposes."

The rockets now brought other men up for interviews with Jonas, men who came up in business suits and who looked sick when they got off the ships. But space had been tamed. They were almost at home in the station, where the air was good and where there was a comfortable gravity, while the walls shut out space. There were conferences and inspections. And finally, Jonas called a meeting of all personnel for the next evening.

His face was serious as he stood up on a table to face the men. He looked from one to another, and finally he started in a voice they had to strain slightly to hear.

"I've got bad news, men! We've decided to abandon the project, effective at once."

There was a gasp, and a milling below him. Jim felt his stomach knot tightly, and tried to raise his voice over the others, but without success. Then they quieted as Jonas held up his hand.

"You won't lose anything. You'll be paid to the end of your contract—not at overtime rates, of course, but in the full normal amount. And you'll be returned to Earth as quickly as possible, free to return to your former life with a nice sum of money to start you out. We don't want to punish anyone. We gambled on being able to finish this station in a year, and we lost. There were a lot of reasons for that, but they can't be helped. We're taking a smaller loss this way, and we can't afford to do anything else. After all, we can't raise taxes to pay for it, as the government can!"

It drew a small laugh, though there were more sick faces than Jim had expected, after the announcement that there would be no loss. Then he remembered that most of the men and women here had come up because they'd had no ties on Earth. They had little to go back to, and they'd built a new way of life here. It was going to be hard for a lot of them to give that up.

"I'm going to propose we draw lots now to see who goes back first," Jonas was saying. "That seems like a fair way. Nora, will you come up here? I've got all the names in a basket . . ."

Jim stood up quietly and moved toward the table where Jonas stood. The man saw him coming and waited quietly, smiling faintly. Jim stared back. He had no idea of how he was going to say what he had to say. He simply moved to the table and climbed up on it.

"If my name's in that box of yours, you can forget it," he said. "I'm not going back!"

There was a gasp from below, but Jonas stood waiting, saying nothing. Nora was shaking her head at Jim, but he disregarded it.

Finally Jonas shrugged. "And just how are you planning to stay?"

He hadn't thought of that. He hadn't thought anything through. But he knew that he had to stay. He swung around to face the others. "We've got contracts for the rest of the time we were supposed to work," he said. "And as long as we're working, they're going to have a hard time kicking us out. Let them try. We're the men who've been rubbing shoulders with the rocket pilots. Do you think any of the rockets would leave the ground if they were told they had to evict us?"

He got no reaction, as he had expected. But he let the words come out that had to come. "Go ahead. Go back to Earth. Go back to stagger around on your hands and knees because you aren't used to the gravity. And go back to watching them laugh at you as the boys who couldn't do a job! I don't care. You'll have money down there. That's all Jonas thinks you came up here for. You'll have a lot of money, for a while. And you can think of some military man busy up here tearing out the laboratories and putting in more bombs. You can have fun, knowing you let something that belonged to all the people turn into nothing but a big battleship in the sky. You let the man who did the most to keep this station going get sacked from his job by Jonas here. Now you might as well go back with him.

"But I'm not going to do it. Until they carry me away from here in chains, I'm sticking. And I'm going to work. I'm going to get up and work for sixteen straight hours. Then I'm going to sleep for eight and do it all over again. And when they do take me down, I'll know I did all I could. I'll be able to think of Bart Smith dying without feeling I let him down completely. It won't do any good. But I'm going to do it. And the rest of you can go back and figure what I think of Jonas' little pets!"

He was crying, and he felt like a fool. It was anger and hate for all the disappointment coming out in him—and it was something more. It was all the frontiers of the future that man would be giving up when he let the division of the station into military and civilian authority lapse.

He stopped, turning to the men once more. "I'm going to be thinking of something else, too. When we picked up Peter Chiam in what some men consider a waste of time and money, his words were, 'Thanks, Yanks. I knew you'd come.' He was a Combine man, but he thought that we could be depended on. I wonder what he'll think when he finds we've decided to quit. Oh, go back to Earth. I'm sick of the lot of you!"

Jonas waited, and the men were quiet. And then suddenly little Terrence Rodriguez let out a yell. "Make it two, Jim!"

Phil Ross had been grinning, as if he'd been watching a stage performance. But he stuck up his own hand. "Three."

"Four," Nora said. She looked unhappy, but she wasn't letting Jim down.

He'd never seen a crowd react before. But now there was suddenly a confusion of hands and yells. Men began jostling forward. And Jonas stepped forward.

"All right," he shouted, his voice suddenly ringing like that of an orator. "All right. Hotheads on the right, the men who are going back on the left. Let's see what's happening."

At first Jim had thought they would all stay. He found that less than half were with him. But it was over two hundred.

Jonas nodded, as they separated. "All right. Jim is right in guessing that I can't force you to go back, but he's forgotten that there are military men who can handle such a situation. But we'll skip that. It will be some time until the new crew could be shipped up. If you want to work, go ahead. But I'll make a proposition. You have to eat, you know. And there isn't enough food here for two months for all of you. So I'm going to charge you three months' salary for the cost of shipping up more—and it's less than the rocket fuel costs, at that. No, wait a minute." He somehow quieted the uproar, and went on. "I know you can't do anything about it, and you know it. But I've got a bargain. If you can prove yourselves the conquering heroes Jim wants to be, you'll get it all back, and twice as much as a bonus. All you have to do is to finish the station within the contract date. That should be safe enough a proposition for my company!"

He laughed at them, dropped from the table, and began issuing numbers to the men who were going back.

Jim stared at him, realizing suddenly that he'd been used! Jonas had never meant to abandon the station without a last desperate attempt. He'd warned Jim he was going to use his hate, and then he'd done it.

Now Jim couldn't tell the men the facts, either—because they had to be working against a dare if they were to avoid being penalized for sticking with him to finish the job.

He looked at the men on his side, though, and couldn't regret it. He'd been himself, however foolish—and he had two hundred friends to prove both Bart and Dan had been right.

"All right," he said quietly. "Let's get to work!"

Chapter 18 Deadline

About twenty of the men changed sides before the rockets could take them back, but Jim and the men he had picked as foremen sent them back. They wanted no doubtful men in the group. They had had time to sober up from the emotions of the meeting, and had looked around to see how impossible the job ahead was going to be.

Two hundred men couldn't do it—and yet they had to do it, not only for the money but for their own respect. They had only one major advantage. Before, the men who had grown listless had cut the pace down for all the others. Now they were all working at full speed. And they had a handicap which made the whole thing impossible. There was no engineer with them.

Then the last rocket up to take off the men who were leaving brought three passengers with it. Dan Bailey and his wife got off, followed by Thorndyke. As Jim shouted and ran toward them, Dan grinned. "Hi, Jim. We heard you needed men. We quit our jobs. Don't blame Gantry, either. After we took care of the guard at the gate, we forced him to bring us up."

His eye closed in a wink, and Jim knew that it had been a general conspiracy. Probably the men at Major Electric were having a good laugh at this further "defiance" of them. But he didn't care.

"Then get to your jobs," he said, while pumping their hands. "And Dan, you're to run the whole works. Mr. Thorndyke, you're not a boss. You told me once why I couldn't be, and you were right. The same shoe fits you now. Dig into those darned blueprints and find out what we're to do, and then let Dan get it done. I've got a taxi to run."

Jim had found another woman who could help Dr. Perez—one of the men who had stayed—and had put Nora to work on the taxi during the hours when he had to sleep. She was doing as well as he could by now, but it was still something he felt responsible for.

Jonas stayed in his own section, except when he felt it wise to come out and sneer good-naturedly at them. But it was impossible to keep hating him. Little by little, he was accepted. They had to have someone to show how much they meant business, and he fitted into the role of a man being shown as easily as if he'd been born for it.

The amount of work was staggering, and some required the knowledge of skilled men they didn't have. At first Jim gave up in despair at the need to install the big radar antenna on the hub. But it turned out conveniently that a man who had come up in uniform during the week was a radar expert, and he managed to get interested in their work and to show them what had to be done in his free time.

Jim ground his teeth at the hypocrisy—and then blessed the fact that it was all a sham. They could never have done anything against real resistance.

The laboratories were being installed as quickly as they could. In the open spaces, where the sheathing of the doughnut wheel had been incomplete, Jim was moving the heavy stuff in directly. It was a rough, nerve-breaking job to match the rotation of the station with the taxi and clamp on while the big equipment was lowered. But it saved time over using the normal entrance through the hub and down the freight elevator.

As fast as a section was finished, scientists came up from Earth and occupied it. At first the men grumbled at this, but in time they took it for granted. And the new men kept carefully out of the way of the workers. Jim found an explanation for it that satisfied everyone—until they finished the station, it looked as if there might be no chance again to use it for civilian work. Naturally, the scientists were taking the brief chance they had—in fact, they were actually cheering the men on.

There was a certain amount of truth in that. A group of the scientists and their helpers were laboriously going out each day and working on the construction of the observatory, which was to float behind the station, and to be connected by loose power and television cables. It was a rough job, and most of them could take only a little of it. But it cut down the impossibility of finishing a trifle.

Jim went to see Halpern himself. The colonel led him back to the private office and closed the door. "What's on your mind, you young rebel? Aside from mutiny!"

"I've been thinking a lot of your personnel look seedy," Jim told him, keeping his face straight. "They don't get any exercise here. I was wondering if we couldn't lend you the services of Dr. Perez to check them over."

Halpern grinned slowly. "And take him out of the kitchen? No. Besides, I can guess what his recommendation would be. He'd decide they needed some fresh space and a lot of exercise. And you know, it's a funny thing, but I've been thinking the same. They should learn to handle themselves out there. I can't tell them what to do with their free time, Jim, and I can't put them on civilian work. But if any should feel like following your suggestion, I'll let them know—unofficially, of course—that you will be happy to see them."

It had been easier than Jim had supposed, though he already felt sure that the military man didn't want to see the station go out of civilian hands and to have to assume sole responsibility.

A few of the military men came out from then on, and joined in the work. They did the rough jobs—and the very skilled ones, since many of them were highly trained technicians.

There were endless details to the station. The trim-system alone was enough to drive men crazy. The station had to be balanced, eventually. To a rough degree, that could be done by storing all heavy material evenly. But when a man walked from one side to the other, it would upset the balance slightly. The station had to rotate evenly and avoid all wobble, if it were to do all the things required of it.

To make balance possible, there were a series of tanks,

pipes and pumps, with automatic controls. If one section had too much mass, the water could be pumped quickly into the opposing side to balance it. It was a maze of parts, however.

The wiring was the worst of all. They had too few trained electricians. Thorndyke put that off for one of the last jobs, using an extra hour each day snatched from their sleep to teach the basic skill to a group of the men.

Jim wasn't getting his eight hours of sleep. He couldn't. He had to drive himself to the edge of collapse before he could relax. And he kept his eye on the production charts. They were doing twice the work that the whole crew had done before, and morale was high. He showed the charts each evening at the one big meal, and the men felt they were making it.

But Jim wasn't so sure. One major accident could set them back enough to overcome all their efforts. And each job was a new challenge. Perez was worried, too. The doctor warned Jim that there was no way of knowing what the effects of fatigue would be under these conditions. The light gravity made it easier to work, but it might also make it easier to go past the stage where exhaustion was dangerous without realizing it.

They were installing one of the big pumps at the end of the first month when the accident happened. Jim saw it coming, and tried to yell a warning, but there was no time. The station wobbled at just the wrong second, and the cable that was already frayed snapped. The pump hit the deck and broke the supports that were still complete. It went through the deck, and then the outer hull. It struck out on its own, keeping the straight line motion that the station's rotation had become the moment it was free.

Jim finally chased it down in the taxi and managed to bring it back. He looked down at the shocked faces of the men, and grinned. His own shock had worn off while he was in the taxi.

"Okay," he called over the phones. "So we've had the accident. Now maybe you butterfingers will stop worrying

151

about preventing it and get down to work. Bill, how's the bracing coming along?"

The big man straightened up from the rush job on the deck braces, and the dark cloud suddenly passed from his face. "It's ready, Jim. But a fine trick it was to be making that accident happen on our shift, just because you couldn't stand the strain of waiting. Eh, boys?"

It was weak repartee, but they didn't care. In the daily strain of living, anything that varied the pace was welcome. Jim managed to laugh, and then leaped out of the taxi and down to help realign the footing for the pump.

There were only two weeks left when Jonas came into the dining room one evening, carrying a group of papers. He threw them down, looking chagrined.

"It looks as if you men may win your bet, after all," he admitted. "At least the company on Earth seems to think so. Well, I won't hold it against you. They've sent up word that the television industries are considering building that station twenty-two thousand miles out again, now that this one is about done. And they've decided to let you have a crack at it, if it comes through. Here, I'm supposed to leave these application blanks for anyone who wants to apply for work on the next station."

There was a concerted dive for the papers, but Jim gathered them up and began passing them out. "They probably figure we'll let down and start mooning about a new job," he said. "But okay, let's all fill the things out. Then we've got work to do."

Jonas grinned at him over the back of the men and went out again.

Jim found Jonas waiting in his cabin when he went to sign his own application. The man took it and tore it up, drawing out another. "I didn't want you to look surprised out there, so I made out a fake for you. You'd better read this," he advised.

Jim frowned and ran through it. Then he saw that it was a contract for a year as foreman—as project foreman. He blinked. "Why?"

"Why? Because you're already that on the books here.

Don't you know it when you take over control of a job?"

Jim hadn't had time to think. He'd been faced with the job of making good on his bluff, and he'd dug into it. Aside from that, he couldn't see that it was any different from the other jobs he'd had to do. Dan, Terrence and Thorndyke had done the actual directing, and he'd been happy to have them doing it. Of course, there had been the conferences at night with them . . .

Jim signed it and handed it back. "So you think we've got a chance?"

"I always thought you had a chance, Jim," Jonas told him. "Not too good a one—but one that had to be taken. Major Electric has had some bad breaks, now that things are in turmoil down there. And paying that penalty clause would just about throw us—while finishing on time would set everything right again. Yes, I think you've got a chance. But I have nightmares every night, because I think it's a mighty slim one. If we do—well, there are all kinds of things, then. But don't count too much on that application, though."

He left, and Jim rolled over, falling asleep at once before he could take off his clothes.

* * * * *

Things were still touch and go when there was only one week left. The men stared at the progress chart grimly. But there was no slackening of work.

They were supposed to finish one year from the beginning of the station—which was the date of the formal signing of the contract. It had been signed on the tenth of October, at noon, Washington time. Jim had the clocks set to Washington time, so that the men could keep accurate track of the work.

The final day came, and with it a group of three men to act as inspectors. They passed through the station slowly, until they came to the unfinished section. All that had to be done was to finish the fabric inner layer, two decks, a wall, and the outer sheathing, or meteor bumper. It had been left till the last, to leave an opening to the outside for the taxi loads. And there was room for no more than thirty men to work.

Jim had let Terrence's men go back, and was standing at the air lock of the taxi, handing out the plates while another man fastened them in place.

"All done in here," Terrence announced. Jim slapped the last plate on, and watched it welded into place.

"What time is it?" he asked. There had been no time to watch the central clock, and he'd deliberately kept the men from knowing what time it was. If they missed, he still wanted the station finished. If they won, the victory would be all the sweeter.

Then he realized there was no radio contact now, with the outer shell completely covered. It shielded the tiny power of his transmitter from reaching the men inside.

He whipped the taxi around and over to its lock, jumped from it, and ran toward the big recreation room.

Jonas was arguing hotly with the three inspectors, while Colonel Halpern stood by, scowling.

The clock stood at twelve twenty-nine. They had missed the deadline by almost thirty minutes!

Jim dropped his shoulders slowly and turned to go, but Jonas called after him. "Wait a minute, Jim! We haven't lost yet. In fact, by common practice, if we finish on the same day, we win."

"You'll have to get a ruling," the head inspector said. "A year is what's called for, not the day on which the year ends. We're ready to okay the station, if you can get an okay on the time."

"A year," Jonas said flatly, "is a lot of things. Look it up in a dictionary. You'll find that an astronomical year is a period of 365 days, 5 hours and 48 minutes plus a few seconds. It's the period required for the Earth to circle the Sun—and the difference is why we have to have leap years to balance things. This is an astronomical object— and I want the benefit of the full astronomical year!"

Halpern reached out for a sheet of paper as a noncom came in. "Maybe this will settle things," he said. "I radioed a report the minute the inspection was finished. Let's see."

He spread it out and they stared down at it, holding their breaths. It was short and direct.

"CONTRACT FULFILLED. CONGRATULATIONS!"

Jonas went through with his act to the final end, publicly standing before the men in the recreation hall and telling them that he'd been wrong. Jim watched him, admiring the man for the sincerity he managed to put into his apology. It left the men feeling that they had really done something beyond their work, and it did Jonas no harm. They might have laughed if he'd confessed that there had been no intention of abandoning the project and that it had all been a glorious swindle; but it wouldn't have been as satisfying to them as watching him apologize.

Then he dug out a bundle of papers, and an announcement. "I have something better than my words," he told them. "I've been in contact with Earth for the last three hours, and I've got a list here. It's a list of the men who are going to work on the television relay station! *We got the contract!*"

They shoved forward, shouting, while Jonas tacked the list to a bulletin board and managed to slip out of the way. Jim pushed forward with the others. He was sure that he'd be accepted. The words of Jonas when he'd been given the special contract had made that seem certain. But he couldn't rest until he found his name printed there.

He stood, staring at the listing. There was a column on each of five sheets of paper—and the numbers indicated that two hundred and eleven men and women had been accepted. Nearly all the men were going to be taken on. There was an entry for Henry Standish and another for Alvin Steadman. But the name of James Stanley wasn't on the list.

He let it sink in slowly. It took time. And the sudden buzz around him showed that the others had noticed it. One of the men let out a yell, and swung him around.

"Jim, we ain't going up there without you! You're coming. Just let them try to stop you."

He shook his head. "Who said I applied for the job, Buck? I've got a college course to finish down on Earth."

They grumbled, and it felt good to him. It wasn't like leaving his job with Griswold. But he couldn't keep up the act in front of them. He swung out, pulling his space suit off a hook in the hub, and moved down toward the taxi. It was one place where he would have a chance to think it out in peace.

"Jim!" It was Nora, and he stopped for her. She came up to him, her face hurt and puzzled. "Jim, I wasn't on the list, either. Neither was Terrence Rodriguez."

"Terry didn't apply," he told her woodenly. "He's staying on at the station, by his own request. He's found a girl, and they'll head the civilian work force here after they're married."

But there was no such reason for not listing Nora and him. He couldn't believe that Jonas would be spiteful, though the man had warned him not to count on his application, now that he thought of it. Probably the order had come from down on Earth. After all, he had been inciting mutiny when he'd sounded off. And Nora had seconded him.

"We'll make out," he told her. "Men are in space now, and we put them there. Isn't that enough? We'll be able to look up here, and know that the Earth is bigger than it used to be because we had a chance to help with this. Let's take a look at it."

The station looked good from half a mile away in the little taxi. It glistened in completeness, and there was no wobble to its spin. Its top faced the Sun, drawing power from the sun mirror trough around it. The hub ran out through the two spokes to the wheel in which men lived and worked. The radar antenna faced Earth, and the observatory trailed along behind.

Jim stared at it, wondering whether everything was actually as wonderful as it looked and as he'd described it. Men were still uncertain, down on Earth.

Yet the tension had let up a little. Perhaps that was because the rescue of the Combine pilots had awakened some sense of common feeling and peril, or perhaps it was because of something entirely different. The first papers that carried the story of the completion had seemed to feel that most of the danger from the station was over, now that it was under the divided command of military and civilian groups, according to the radio messages that had been received.

At least there would never again be a race to build another station. The trip to rescue the Combine men had proved that an operating station could protect itself from any other attempt with no difficulty. From the station, any place on its orbit was comparatively easy to reach, either for rescue or attack.

If the science Jim hoped to see developed here, along with the riches it could bring, never were paid for by arrogance and abuse of the military power, all would be fine. But he couldn't be sure. Having a weapon of such overwhelming force in the hands of any one nation was a terrible temptation—and could lead to an endless hatred from other nations that would make it necessary to use its power.

Somehow, in spite of all their dreams, the station wasn't enough. Men couldn't solve all their problems by leaving them to a few men up there.

He saw Mark's rocket coming up from Earth and headed the taxi in. The pilot brought the big ship up beside the station with a smoothness that could never have been achieved at the beginning, and Jim ran the taxi into the air lock.

Mark came out with a grin over his thin face, and a tissue edition of a newspaper in his hand. "Jim, you did it! You got it done, and it's a honey of a job. Here!"

Jim opened the paper, wondering what could be so important, while Nora took the taxi controls. Then he whistled. The World Congress had met in a body and had voted unanimously to congratulate the United States on the completion of the station. And it had been the Combine delegate who had proposed the motion. The same delegate had offered to make available all Combine knowledge on atomic rockets in return for the right to send a few of their scientists to the station for some experiments that could be made nowhere else.

The United States had made no mention of having the secrets already, or clues enough to find them. It had accepted.

"Sweetness and light!" Jim said.

He still couldn't be sure, though he felt better. It was probably a deliberate move by the Combine, now afraid to let all the scientific progress possible through the station go to an opposing power. It almost surely was inspired more by worry than by good will. Yet out of such moves, good will could grow.

Jim had resigned himself to his failure to win a position on the second station when he came back into the recreation hall. He turned to find a seat and listen to the radio broadcasts, drawing Nora with him.

But before he could sit down, Jonas and Halpern pounced on him and Nora, dragging the two of them aside into Jonas' office.

"Where've you been?" the man cried. "Jim, I've been hunting the station high and low for you. Mark Emmett! Hey, Mark!"

Jim had dashed to the door, and now came back, dragging the grinning pilot after him.

"Did you bring it up, Mark?"

Mark nodded, and dragged a thin case from his suit, handing it over. Jonas beamed, and pulled a sheet of parchment out of it, staring at it fondly. Then he handed it to Jim.

It was a beautifully engraved thing, but the words blurred as Jim began to read. "This will certify that James Stanley, having passed all courses and tests, and having qualified by ability and experience, is hereby licensed to operate and to assume command of any vessel powered by chemical rockets for use in or beyond the atmosphere of Earth, and that . . ."

Nora took it from him and stood staring at it, her face slowly breaking into an inner glow that seemed to radiate around the room. "Jim! This means . . ."

"It means more than that," Colonel Halpern broke in, before she could finish. "It means that in less than a year, we're going to be taking off on the first trip to the Moon. We've already signed more contracts with Major Electric for that, and we've got the plans ready. You two are going along. And Jim, you've been picked as chief pilot."

Jim sat down slowly, trying to believe the words he was hearing. "But I thought, when I was turned down for the second station—"

"Turned down?" Jonas grunted as if hit by a fist. "Jim, I meant to pull a big surprise party, and I guess I muffed it by waiting too long, if you thought that. You were moved over to a bigger job, man. Don't you realize you've had more experience in fancy maneuvering in space than all the other pilots combined? We had to have you. And because we don't want to break up a good team, we're shipping Nora along as your copilot. There's room on the Moon for women as well as men, I guess."

Jim's mind seized on the last sentence. Room for women as well as men—and for every race and country. He'd overlooked that in his worrying. He'd forgotten that the space station had always been just a step to space—the real space that could never be fully conquered. Men would have a frontier to take their energies, and to broaden their horizons. There would be no sense in fighting over a space station when there were all the planets beyond it. And there would be no use in trying to conquer the world with the station, when those planets were stronger than any single man-made structure could ever be. The station was only a step—and what lay beyond was the real future.

"Space has its own rules," Colonel Halpern said slowly. "Jim, on Earth you were just a kid—a lonely kid who was growing bitter and drawing into himself. Out here, you've turned into a man! It isn't just skill we need for the Moon trip. It's men who have the right stuff in them. That's why we picked you—because you're that kind of man. Mark, Jonas, come on. Let's let them get used to the idea."

The men filed out of the office. At the door Mark turned and grinned at the two. And his words were almost the same as those with which he had first greeted Jim on the original trip into space.

"Welcome, spacemen!"

Spacemen! Jim smiled slowly, turning to see Nora smiling back at him.

Someday the whole race of men would be spacemen. This was only the beginning.